Dedication

For my brother, Tim. The song of his life has made me a better writer.

Killer Storms

Phil Walker

Table of Contents

Chapter 1   Monsters of Mother Nature
Chapter 2   Sounding the Alarm
Chapter 3   Packing Up
Chapter 4   No Time to Lose
Chapter 5   Running
Chapter 6   The Road to Hell
Chapter 7   Struggling for Safety
Chapter 8   Home, not so sweet, Home
Chapter 9   Dark Forecasts
Chapter 10   Insights
Chapter 11   Holly's Howling Winds
Chapter 12   Digging In
Chapter 13   Refugees
Chapter 14   Thinking Ahead
Chapter 15   Sanctuary
Chapter 16   Hard Reality
Chapter 17   Searching the Neighborhood
Chapter 18   Additional Reconnaissance
Chapter 19   More Survivors
Chapter 20   Overloaded
Chapter 21   Damn, Dam
Chapter 22   Soaked and Miserable
Chapter 23   Escape to the Roof
Chapter 24   Catastrophe
Chapter 25   Fighting to Survive
Chapter 26   A New Dawn

Killer Storms

Chapter 1
Monsters of Mother Nature

<u>Sunday Night</u>

Doctor Aaron Colson threw his pen on the desk in frustration as he stared at the TV. A Category 5, hurricane was churning toward Florida and would slam the east coast at 156 miles per hour in no more than forty-eight hours. The storm was drawing a bead on his front door. Still, there was more.

He had not spent a lifetime as a meteorologist, without learning when the people were not telling the whole story. This was either because they didn't know or because their suspicions were not certainties. In this case, there was a certainty. Hurricane Karl would make landfall on the Space Coast in two days. However, Aaron suspected something else was on the mind of the current senior analyst of the Weather Channel's Evan Driscoll.

Evan had been Aaron's protégé at the Weather Channel in Atlanta and had moved into the senior slot when Aaron retired a few years ago. Now, here he was, speaking seriously of the threat of this monster storm. Yesterday, the governor of Florida had issued mandatory evacuations for the Space Coast from Melbourne to St. Augustine, beginning with the barrier islands.

Yet, Aaron knew Evan left something unsaid.

Aaron continued to watch and listen in the office of his home in The Villages. The local radio station broadcast a steady stream of evacuation alerts, advisories and warnings to the people of the sprawling retirement community. Turning away from the Weather Channel, Aaron pulled up multiple images from the National Hurricane Center on his computer.

A woman's voice spoke behind him. "What's the latest?"

Aaron looked up at his wife, Angie, standing in the double doors. He could always count on her to stay calm in any situation.

Aaron loved her for that and so much more. "Karl is definitely going to make landfall on the Space Coast. It'll come ashore as a Cat 5 storm. The governor is ordering mandatory evacuations."

"What about us?"

"We're over a hundred miles from the coast. Historically, The Villages has ridden out hurricanes without suffering catastrophic damage. Our community is better prepared to stand up to a disaster than anywhere else in the state."

"I'm pretty sure you didn't answer my question."

"The evacuation orders are not mandatory for The Villages but a good number of people are leaving. Traffic on I-75 northbound is already heavy. My gut feeling is to stay put. Our planning for storms like this is better than most. I think it will be enough."

Angie leaned against the door frame. "Okay. How long before Karl gets here?

"Two days."

"Are you going to come to bed?"

"In a few minutes. I've been watching Evan Driscoll. I'm going to call Atlanta and try and talk to him. Something besides Karl is going on."

Angie crossed her arms. "He looks a little busy right now. I bet he won't take your call."

"It's worth a try. Maybe he'll tell me something that isn't going out over the air." Aaron picked up his phone and punched Evan's personal number.

It rang a few times, before a familiar voice answered. "I might have known you couldn't help sticking your nose into this."

"Hey, that storm in the Atlantic is heading straight at me."

"It's really a big one. An unusual track too. Karl will go north of the Bahamas and plow right into the Space Coast. I can't imagine it getting any stronger. It's been a Cat 5 storm for three days. You and your neighbors are in for a rough ride, Aaron. Wait a minute, I'll put John Meyers on with us."

A few seconds later, John joined the call. "Hi Aaron, get the hell outta there. Come stay at my house."

"I've been listening to the local radio station. I-75 is a mess from people around here leaving, along with the overflow traffic from the East Coast. I don't want to risk getting caught up in that. My house is safer than my car. Besides, Karl might turn north once it hits the Florida coast."

"Unlikely," cautioned Evan. "A dome of high pressure over the southeast states will likely keep Karl headed for you."

John joined in. "Orlando is right in the bullseye. Even though it's forty miles from the coast, Karl could still be Cat 3 or even 4 when it rolls in there. It'll shred Mickey Mouse to confetti. People are leaving. Would you believe it, a lot of them are headed south to Miami, which will not be effected?"

Aaron looked again at the images from the Hurricane Center. "Karl is moving so slowly it will weaken crossing the Florida peninsula and probably blow itself out before it reaches the west coast."

"If nothing else happens." Evan's tone was less convincing.

Did I hear an 'also' in your last update? You didn't say anything on the air but how about telling me what you think you see."

"We have another Cat 5 hurricane whipping away in the Caribbean. Can you pull it up from the NHC?"

Aaron clicked his monitor and got the image. "So?"

"When was the last time we had two hurricanes of such intensity at the same time?"

Aaron looked at the pictures. "Let's see. That storm's name is Holly but according to what I'm seeing it's been tracking due west since it cleared Barbados and passed north of Jamaica. It's a killer but all the models say it will continue west and hit the Yucatan."

"Every model but one." Evan took a deep breath. "That model shows Holly making a wide turn to the north putting Cuba right in the bullseye and then on to the west coast of Florida. What would happen if Karl were to cross the state, come out on the Gulf side and mix with Holly?"

"The Fujiwara effect?"

"Exactly. Having two huge hurricanes dancing around each other, so close to major population centers would be a real disaster. If they combine it could produce the 'Mother of all Storms' and slam ashore somewhere between Tampa to New Orleans."

"I understand you worrying. But Evan, the likelihood of anything like that happening has got to be remote."

"Right now, the probability is less than five percent."

"Maybe you're overthinking this."

"I hope so. Anyway, it's almost midnight. The National Hurricane Center won't have another update until six a.m. John and I are going to have a decent meal and grab some sleep."

"Yeah," John chimed in, "We'll have a better picture in the morning."

"Things are likely to get incredibly hectic for you but, if you can, I'd like to be kept in the loop."

"You still know more about the Fujiwara effect than anyone. We may need you later. Gotta go." The line went dead.

Aaron sat back in his chair and looked at his wife. "You heard him on the speaker. I knew Evan was thinking about something else."

"Feel better now?"

"I'm glad I know what's going on but now I'm worried." He pointed to the screen. "Holly is a much more compact hurricane and moving two or three times as fast as Karl."

"Can we go to bed now? They said they won't know more till morning."

Aaron switched off the television and radio and turned off the light.

❖

<u>**Monday Morning**</u>

The phone rang and rang in Evan Driscoll's apartment. He groped for it in the dark and almost shouted into the receiver. "What is it?"

"I'm very sorry to wake you, Dr. Driscoll. The newest models on the storms are out from the National Hurricane Center. The director says you need to come in as soon as possible."

"Did you call John?"

"Yes, and several others."

"Has something happened?" Evan fumbled for the switch on his table lamp and sat up.

"I'm only an operator, sir. I haven't been told anything else, except to call you."

"Alright. Tell the director I'll be in as quickly as possible."

Forty-five minutes later, Evan pulled into his spot in the parking garage. John Meyers drove in right behind him.

Driscoll slammed the car door. "If I'd known they would need us so soon, we could have stayed in the hotel across the street. Have you heard what this is about?"

"I called the studio on the way in. The relief meteorologist said it would be better if we saw the latest images ourselves."

"For heaven's sake, John, what's so important to get us out of bed and then clam up."

"We're gonna find out."

The two men went up the elevator and down a hallway to the studio. There were more people than usual clustered in small groups, especially at this early hour, moving around and studying banks of video monitors. As they came in, one of the line producers walked up.

"Sorry to roust you so early. The new models are in from the NHC. You need to see this."

Evan sat down and stared at the big monitor. The screen showed a broad view of the Atlantic Ocean, the Florida peninsula, and the Gulf of Mexico. Karl continued to churn ponderously toward the Space Coast. The picture in the Caribbean had a much different picture.

John leaned over Evan's shoulder, "What the hell?"

"Holly has made a looping right-hand turn to the north of Jamaica and into the Gulf. Let's see what the models say now." He punched in letters and numbers. The new models showed Holly with a half a dozen tracks spread out in a fan from New Orleans to Tampa.

John stood up and put his hand to his mouth. "I hope this isn't going to be another Katrina."

"Or worse. Two of these models have Holly coming ashore on the west coast of Florida." He typed more entries. "It's moving along almost thirty miles an hour. At that rate, it will make landfall in two days."

"With Karl still churning in the Atlantic, and a hurricane warning in effect for the Space Coast and Orlando, people are scrambling to evacuate the area.

"But there haven't been any warnings for the west coast. Even if the governor gave the order immediately, there would hardly be enough time for people to run for safety. To say nothing of the congestion on the highways from people trying to evacuate from both coasts."

"We don't know if Holly will even impact Florida. What if the governor puts out an emergency message and the storm doesn't hit the state at all?"

"It's a tough call. We're going to have to coordinate with NHC and give him the best data we can. The next few hours will tell us a lot."

"Like you said, Evan, if he gave the order to evacuate western Florida right now, there would be little time for anyone to react. Waiting even a few hours could make the panic as bad as the storm when people realize they are going to be trapped in their cars."

"Not as bad as doing nothing. Karl will hit the Space Coast in two days. The prediction is better than an even chance these two storms will collide and become one colossal storm."

"I can't imagine. It would be unprecedented. The damage would be catastrophic and the loss of lives could run into the thousands."

A staffer approached the two. "Dr. Driscoll, there's a call for you from the Governor of Florida."

John waved his hands. "Why do you suppose he wants to talk with you? He must have already spoken to the NHC."

"Offhand I would say the governor is looking for a second opinion. In any case, he would need us to help facilitate a mass evacuation." Evan turned to the staffer. "What line?"

"Line three."

Evan tapped a key and simultaneously hit the speaker button. "Good morning, Governor. This is Evan Driscoll. My colleague John Meyers is on speaker with us. How can we help?"

The governor's voice had a measured, calm quality barely covering the magnitude of the crisis. "Good morning, Dr. Driscoll. I've been speaking with the National Hurricane Center. They tell me there's a better than a one in four chance this storm in the Gulf could bend east and strike the west coast. Is that also your assessment?"

"Yes, it is, Governor. We are faced with the possibility both Karl and Holly could merge over the Florida peninsula. "

"Does that shit really happen?"

"All the time, Governor. There are dozens of documented instances where two hurricanes come together. This would be the first time in our neighborhood."

"I was afraid you were going to say that. The NHC told me the same thing. There's even a name for it."

"Right, the Fujiwara effect. Named for the Japanese scientist who first described it."

"I have to decide whether to issue additional evacuation

orders for the west coast. How long before you can say this is the real deal?"

"We've been talking about that. If you're going to make the call, you must do it in the next few hours. Even then, it will be a mad rush for people to move to safety."

"Don't I know it? Okay. Let's set noon today as the drop-dead hour. Even if you're still not sure of Holly's track, I'm going to err on the side of caution."

"That's what I would do, Governor. I'll call you back."

Evan clicked off the call and looked at his friend. "Well, you and I will have to make the most important weather forecast of our lives."

Chapter 2
Sounding the Alarm

<u>**Monday morning**</u>

Aaron was back in his home office by five a.m. Despite being retired, he still rose early, and liked the two or three hours of solitude before Angie got up. When he turned on all the communications systems, he realized things had changed. The Weather Channel had the latest.

… the next update from the National Hurricane Center is due at six a.m., but we are already getting early reports that the storm track of another Category 5 hurricane, Holly, shifted dramatically overnight and is moving north, directly toward Cuba, and on a track, to impact states along the Gulf of Mexico.

Aaron stared at the television. "Terrific. So much for low probabilities." He went to the kitchen to make a cup of coffee. While it brewed, he stepped outside to collect the newspaper from the driveway.

Returning to the kitchen, he put cream in the coffee and carried it to the office tossing the newspaper aside and sipping the coffee. The local radio station was broadcasting nothing but coverage of the approaching Atlantic hurricane and checklists of things people should do to prepare for the storm. Aaron compared that with his own preparations.

He had a generator installed outside next to the garage to provide minimum electrical needs. Inside the garage, an entire wall was covered with built-in wooden cubicles. Inside them were boxes bulging with supplies: medical and first aid basics, two-way radios, several lanterns with spare batteries, rows of food, twenty cases of bottled water, even a large tent. Over the past several years, Aaron accumulated these provisions, bit by bit. He felt sure nothing was missing. If an emergency of any kind occurred, he had it covered.

The coffee was cold by the time Aaron finished running the checklist in his mind. He scooped up his cup, went to the kitchen and heated it up in the microwave, carrying it back to the office. It didn't take long to catch up on the new forecasts. The National Hurricane Center had released the latest group of models with possible storm tracks for Holly. In the past six hours the hurricane shifted to the north and east. It was spilling into the Gulf of Mexico at thirty miles an hour. The models were all over the place, like the fingers of a hand, pointing at the gulf coast of the United States. Even more disturbing, two of those models showed Holly bending further east with landfall somewhere between Naples and Tampa on the west Florida coast.

Aaron concentrated on the Weather Channel. It was no surprise to see Evan Driscoll back in the studio running through the probabilities for all the storm tracks. Evan always spoke in a calm and deliberate manner, but Aaron heard the tension in his voice. With a couple of keystrokes, the real time images from the NHC came on the computer.

An hour later, when Angie got up and came into his office with a cup of coffee of her own, he knew a good deal more.

"Anything new?"

"Lots happened overnight. Evan's instincts about Hurricane Holly are turning out to be right. It's coming out of the Caribbean and into the Gulf with only Cuba to slow it down."

Angie sat on the couch and sipped her coffee. "Would you turn down some of this noise? I can hardly hear you."

"Sorry." Aaron switched the TV to mute and turned down the radio.

"That's better. What's going on with the other hurricane?"

"Karl is tracking dead-on toward the Space Coast. It continues as a Cat 5 storm and people are hurrying to get out of its way. It'll come ashore in under thirty-six hours."

"So, that means we have two big hurricanes on a collision course at each other?"

"Exactly. Two of the storm track models have Holly continuing to turn east and hit Florida. We could have two hurricanes hit both coasts at the same time. It's not a sure thing yet. It's too soon to accurately predict Holly's path but the Weather Channel has both Evan and John back in the studio."

There were two things Aaron liked most about Angie. She didn't spook easily and matched his skill at analyzing problems and situations.

Angie looked over his shoulder at the TV screen. "How long before we know more?"

"The next few hours will make the picture clearer." Aaron turned the sound back up on the TV.

The two watched the weather news long enough to become acquainted with the complete picture. Aaron turned back to Angie. "Time to start making some storm preparations of our own."

Aaron went outside and began hauling potted plants, patio furniture or anything else into the garage which might become a projectile in heavy winds. Angie checked the food supplies, making a list of things to buy at the store. After Aaron came in and took a shower, he grilled some hamburgers on the patio grill. Then the two sat down for a quiet late lunch.

The beeping of an alert horn on the television got their attention again. They carried their plates into the office and listened to the announcer give new details.

Because of the developing emergency with Hurricane Holly, the Governor of Florida has issued this advisory for residents of the west coast of Florida. Aaron cranked up the sound on the TV and turned down the radio. The face of the governor came on the screen.

My fellow Floridians. During the last few hours, the National Hurricane Center updated its estimates for Hurricane Holly. This storm made a dramatic shift to the north and east and is a growing threat. It will impact

the west coast of Florida in the next thirty-six hours.
Holly is a Category 5 storm, like Karl, nearly as large,
and moving at twenty-five miles per hour. Holly will pass
over Cuba, near Havana and then continue north.
Passing over Cuba it will slow and weaken, but still poses
a threat to Florida. In the Atlantic, Hurricane Karl
matches Holly's ferocity. It will make landfall on the
Space Coast also in less than thirty-six hours. Mandatory
evacuations are now well underway. Because of the
unprecedented increase in danger from two massive
storms approaching Florida, I feel it necessary to issue
additional evacuation warnings for all citizens living on
the west coast of the state from Tampa to Naples. Take
these advisories very seriously and prepare to leave
immediately. The Florida National Guard is moving
equipment, fuel, medical supplies and personnel into
positions along the evacuation routes to provide aid and
assistance.**

Angie put her hand gently on Aaron's chest. "I can taste the
salt in the air. I hope you're right about this being a safe place to
ride out a storm. In any case, it's a lot safer for Sandy and Mason
here then smack on the coast in Punta Gorda."

"I'd better call her right away." Aaron picked up the phone
and put it on speaker.

"Hi Dad, what's up?"

"Did you see the governor's announcement a few minutes
ago?"

"Nope. We've been busy. What did he say?"

"He said Hurricane Holly has changed direction and is now
expected to smack you on the chin in Punta Gorda."

"Is it a sure thing?"

"Enough for him to order evacuation of the west coast for
everyone north of Naples."

"What about you, Dad, you're north of Naples?"

"You two are safer here than on the coast."

"What about the other hurricane, what's its name, everybody has talked about for a week?"

"Karl. It's still headed right at the Space Coast, but we're a long way inland. Maybe the worst of it will blow out before it gets to us."

"Really Dad, we get stirred up every year over these storms and most of the time it's no big deal."

Angie looked at her husband and her eyebrows shot up. "Listen Sandra, the governor would not be telling everyone to evacuate if he didn't think the threat was real. You should take this more seriously."

"Come on, Mom. We're not retired like you. We have a business to run and a living to make."

Aaron leaned closer to the phone. "That restaurant of yours is right on Charlotte Harbor. If Holly rolls in there, you won't have a restaurant. We can replace a building, but we can't replace you or Mason. Holly will hit the coast in thirty-six hours or less. The outer bands will start to impact you sooner than that. When people realize this is a real emergency, there will be a mad rush to get out. You sure don't want to be caught up with a million panic-stricken people."

There was silence on the other end of the phone. Finally, Sandy came back. "Alright. Mason and I will catch up on the latest news and decide if we need to do something. I'll call you back later today."

She hung up abruptly.

Aaron shrugged his shoulders. "She acts like we were giving her a teenage curfew."

"You raised her to think for herself."

"The operative word is think—coherently, clearly. Sandy has that restaurant shoved so far up her priority list she isn't properly considering the real danger."

"Maybe when we talk to her later, she'll have done that."

Aaron spent the rest of the day monitoring the NHC website, the Weather Channel and the local Villages radio station. With each update the news grew grimmer. When he couldn't stand it any longer, he called his daughter.

Chapter 3
Packing Up

<u>Monday night</u>

The phone rang at the front counter of the restaurant. "Good evening, The Tides Fine Dining, this is Sandy. How may I be of service?"

"Is there something wrong with your cell phone?"

"Oh hi, Dad. I left it in the office. Sorry I didn't call back. We've been busy today. We couldn't run a regular schedule. Most of our suppliers are closed, but we've still been serving what we could, mostly to our regulars. People dashed in all day, looking for something to eat. At the same time, the staff helped Mason put up the storm shutters."

"Good for you. That sounds like you've gotten the message."

"It's been hectic. Between serving cheeseburgers and hearing the news I'm frazzled."

"Okay, I'll make this short. I think you should pack up and head for The Villages as soon as you can."

"The announcements about evacuating are only advisories. It's not a sure thing Holly is going to hit Florida at all."

"A lot has changed in the past several hours. I'm surprised people aren't talking about it."

"They are. Some of the old-timers say they've been through hurricanes before and are going to stay. Maybe we can too."

"Are you willing to bet your life on that?"

"Oh, for heaven's sake, Dad."

"In a very short time the hustle-bustle you're seeing is going to turn into panic. You need to be gone before that happens."

"You're scaring me."

"Good. Yank your head out of the sand. Pay attention to the hell coming at you."

"Hey Dad, mind your own damn business. We've got our hands full here."

Right then, Sandy's friend Amy Kincaid pulled open the front door and rushed in. Fear filled her eyes. She stumbled and grabbed the reception desk to keep from going down.

"Shit, girl. We're from the Midwest where we have tornadoes. Hurricanes happen to someone else. I've seen storms before but never felt Mother Nature was trying to rip me a new one."

Oh boy, maybe dad's, right? Do we need to get the hell out of here?

Sandy waved her hand. "Just a minute, Amy." She held up the phone. "I'm talking to my Dad in The Villages." She returned the phone to her ear. "Okay Dad, you got my attention. I'll talk to Mason. I promise to call you back soon."

"You do that, sweetie."

Before Sandy could put down the phone, Amy moved closer. "That hurricane is going to hit us. I watched the news all day. We should leave, but I have no idea where to go."

"Let's go back and talk to Mason. We'll see if he's as scared of this storm as you are."

They walked back to the kitchen.

Mason and another cook were looking at a wall-mounted television. "Hi Amy, some fun, huh?"

"Stop it. Stop it. Stop it." Amy put her face in her hands, crying into them. Then she screamed at Mason. "This isn't fun. I'm so scared I can't think."

Mason walked over and put his hand on her shoulder. "I'm sorry. Bad joke."

Amy wiped her tears. "The governor says we should get the hell out of here."

"Maybe he's right. What do you think, Sandy?"

"Dad says we should be headed for The Villages before now. I haven't been watching the news. What's happening?"

"Holly's eye hit Havana straight on, tearing Cuba to shreds. The whole damn country is devastated. Now it's entering the Gulf. The Weather Channel says it's regaining strength over the warm water."

"Is it going to hit us?"

"Every hour it looks more like a bullet with our name on it. It's coming, honey."

Sandy looked out the window. "It's raining and the wind's blowing like a freight train."

The Weather Channel flashed a special bulletin. Dr. Evan Driscoll came on screen.

We continue to track the incredible shift of Hurricane Holly to the north and east. The models are now showing landfall near Punta Gorda less than a day from now. The storm continues as a Category 5 hurricane with sustained winds over 150 miles per hour. The outer bands are drenching the state with gale winds making the situation extremely dangerous. We can't escape the fact that two Category 5 storms will ravage central Florida. We have no experience for such an event. Perhaps worse, we cannot forecast the results if these two storms collide. Hurricane lose strength rapidly over land but that might not be the case this time.

Driscoll paused for a moment holding his hand to his ear bud.

We've received word the Governor of Florida has called another press conference which we now join.

The Governor of Florida appeared on the screen. There was activity all over the room as he stood up to the lectern and spoke into the microphone.

To the people of the state of Florida. The latest weather forecasts are in. Hurricane Karl continues as a Category 5 storm in the Atlantic. It will make landfall

along the Space Coast sometime tomorrow night, where mandatory evacuations are now in progress. Hurricane Holly, now past Cuba, where they have twenty-five confirmed fatalities and damage to Havana is extensive, is now in the Gulf and strengthening. The National Hurricane Center says it will hit the west coast of the state in under twenty hours. My previous evacuation advisory for the west coast from Port Charlotte to Tampa is now mandatory.

There's no time to lose. Stop what you're doing and leave now."

The group watched other state officials come forward with maps and charts showing evacuation routes and emergency information.

Mason broke the silence. "No more question of what we do next. Call your Dad back and tell him we're on our way."

Sandy headed back to the dining room. "I'll lock up, double check the shutters and then head home to pack."

Amy grabbed at Sandy's arm. "Hey. Wait a minute. What about me?"

Sandy put a warm hand on her friend's shoulder. "Don't worry. You and Ben are coming with us to The Villages. You should call and tell him. Where is he right now?"

"Still at the hospital. His shift in the pharmacy ended hours ago. Probably all the other nurses are still working too. I've no idea what kind of mess he has."

"Whatever it is, he needs to get out of there along with everyone else. Ask him put together some medical supplies, anything we might need for an emergency. You go home and pack up."

"I'll call Ben and fill him in. When do we leave?"

Sandy looked at her watch. "It's ten o'clock. Can you come to our house in an hour?"

Amy clenched her fists. "I don't know if we can make it. Oh,

I'm so scared. We gotta make it. Don't go without us. Please wait. Wait for us."

Sandy held the front door open for Amy. She couldn't even see into the bay. When she turned back, the staff stood facing her, their eyes big, mouths open.

"If this place is still standing after the storm, you will still have jobs. Now get the hell out of here and go take care of your families."

When the last were gone, Sandy went back to the kitchen to check on Mason.

He was filling large coolers with meat and other perishables from the freezer. "We can't take everything to your dad's house but what we have here will feed a crowd for a while."

"I'm finished up front."

"Why don't you go on home and pack for me? I'll be along shortly. Here, take the receipts with you."

Sandy shouldered her oversized purse and grabbed an umbrella as she went out the back door. The rain smacked her before she took two steps. The wind yanked away her umbrella and bent the rain sideways. She needed two hands to hold the car door open. When she got inside, the wind slammed it shut.

Traffic clogged the road. Sandy plodded along at five miles an hour. The roads leading to the freeway were hopelessly congested. As she drove, Sandy called her father. He answered on the first ring.

"We have the restaurant boarded up. Mason is packing some coolers. I'm going home now to pack some bags. We are bringing another couple with us. I hope you don't mind."

"We can manage. The governor has redirected all the lanes on I-75 northbound for the evacuation. But it's a parking lot. You should take Highway 27. Probably less traffic and it's farther inland. When are you going to leave?"

"About an hour, I think."

"Not later than that, Sandy. Holly's eye is now about

eighteen hours from you, but the outer bands of the storm will hit the coast sooner than that."

"They already have."

"If you leave by midnight it will take three hours to drive here under the best conditions. The important thing is to keep moving and watch out for the ninety-seven thousand nut jobs on the road with you."

"I'm starting to feel like I'm one of the nut jobs."

"No, you're not, but you need to be very careful. People are close to panicking. They are capable of anything. Do you have a gun?"

"We have a Glock, semi-automatic."

"Take it with you, along with all your ammunition."

"Are you kidding? I'm not going to shoot anyone."

"Unless they start shooting at you."

"Have we come to that?"

"Who knows? When something like this happens, people can be incredibly brave or become monsters. It's better to be prepared."

"I should have listened to you earlier. Tell me more about what's happening."

"In addition to Holly rolling in to deliver a first-class punch on the west coast, Hurricane Karl is going to make landfall on the east coast. If they combine anywhere near us, we could be in real trouble."

"You mean in The Villages?"

"That's right. We're caught between two storms."

"Then why are we coming there?"

"Because you'll still be safer here than where you are. The biggest killer in hurricanes is the coastal storm surge. We won't have that here."

Sandy mopped at her hair with a towel. "Okay. We're leaving in an hour, four of us. Pray for us, Daddy. I love you."

"Call or text me as often as you can during the drive. I need to know you guys are all right."

"I'll do that." She punched off the phone, drove the car into the garage, and walked into the house.

Like her father, Sandy talked out loud to herself when she was alone. "Idiot. The suitcases are in the garage. You walked right past them."

For the next hour she packed two bags choosing only the most functional clothing for her and Mason. "We ain't going to a celebrity ball. Better grab the go-bag."

She covered the bed with clothing, bath items, prescriptions and other medical supplies.

Sandy emptied a gym bag in the closet and tossed it on the bed. She picked through her purse and pulled out a wallet. She tossed her credit cards and a couple bank bags filled with the cash receipts from three days at the restaurant into the bag. It amounted to several thousand dollars. The sight of the money made Sandy remember her father's words about how crazy, panic-stricken people could act.

She crossed to the nightstand by the bed and took the Glock out of the drawer. It was in a holster with a full box of bullets next to it. Sandy grimly put it into the gym bag on top of the money.

When the suitcases were full, she threw the bag over her shoulder, rolled the luggage to the garage and opened the door. Then she pulled out a folding chair and sat down, staring out into the night. The wind seemed stronger, blowing the rain in sheets.

Sandy fished the cell phone from her pocket and punched up Amy's number.

It rang several times before she answered. "I've been listening for your call but I had to hunt for my phone."

"I'm all packed here. Did Ben get home?"

"No. I haven't talked with him since I told him we were going with you and to pack some medical supplies. I'm alone here."

"Take it easy. He'll call you as soon as he can. Have you got a couple bags packed?"

"Yeah, sort of." She started to cry. "I don't know what to pack."

Amy's sobs made it hard for Sandy to understand her. "Only pack clothes you can work in, get dirty in, and don't care if you throw away when this is over."

More sniffling at the other end.

"Aaaammy. Listen to me. You gotta get moving. Ben will be home soon. You need to be ready to go with clothing packed for both of you. When Mason gets home, he's gonna want to leave. We need to get on the road as soon as we can. So, blow your nose and get your shit together."

There was silence for a few seconds before Amy cleared her throat. "It's scary being alone. I guess I needed to talk with someone. Thanks. I can do this."

"That's better. Have Ben call me the minute he gets home."

Sandy hung up and called her husband's cell.

He answered on the second ring. "Hi. I'm leaving. You ready?"

"Yes, I called Amy. She's a mess but I think she'll be all right until Ben gets home."

"You know we can't wait on them or at least not long."

"Amy remembered to tell Ben he should pack some medical supplies. We might need them, and him, if it gets rough."

"Honey, we have to get on the road."

Sandy sighed into the phone as the rain continued to fall. "Yeah, I know." The rain peppered the windows hard enough she thought they would break. She looked along the house. The gutters were overflowing.

Chapter 4
No Time to Lose

Amy Kincaid tried to concentrate on packing a bag for her and Ben. The wind and rain hammered against the window. The groan of the rattling window frame, unnerved her. She'd heard windows shake before in the Midwest but always knew the storm would pass. This storm was only beginning.

She frantically flipped hangars in her closet, trying to find clothes to pack. Even this simple job was challenging. Before long, piles of clothing covered the floor with little of it getting into the suitcases.

When the rising wind shook her windows again, Amy slid down to the floor and leaned against the bed. She put her hands to her face and covered her ears to suffocate the sound.

The front door slammed. She jumped to her feet and ran into the hall, plowing into her husband.

"Easy, honey." Ben wrapped his arms around her. "I'm sorry. This was a soon as I could get here. They're evacuating the hospital and I needed to help with that."

Amy sobbed in her husband's shoulder. "I was so afraid, being alone."

"Well, I'm here now. Have you packed?"

"I've been trying."

"Let's go finish up."

The two walked back to the bedroom. Amy wiped away her tears. "I got out a lot of stuff but I didn't know what to pack."

Ben looked around the room, rummaging through the clothes and throwing them on the bed. "Here, pack this stuff."

He separated some jeans, shorts, t-shirts, underwear and socks. Amy half folded and threw them in the bags. She went to the bathroom and came back with two small satchels of toiletries. In minutes the bags were full. Ben zippered them shut and pulled both bags toward the door.

"Sandy said to call her as soon as you got home."

Ben took his phone from a pocket and pushed some buttons. He put it on the speaker as the phone rang. Sandy answered it almost at once. "Hi, Ben. Are you home?"

"A few minutes ago."

"Good. Mason called. He left the restaurant headed home. How soon can you leave to come over here?"

"I'll throw the bags into the SUV, and we can go."

"How's Amy?"

"I'm doing fine now, Ben's here."

"Oh hi, Amy. Move along and hustle over to my house."

Ben's nod comforted her. "We'll be there in a few minutes."

"Really, I'm okay. I'm sorry about the way I'm acting. I'm ashamed of myself. We're leaving now."

"Fine. We need to hit the road headed north as soon as we can."

Sandy put the phone down, leaned back in the chair and stared out through the open garage. The leaden sky, illuminated with flashes of lightning, pressed down. The rain, driven by the wind, was falling in torrents.

There was nothing else to do but wait and run a checklist on her phone until Mason got there. Their home was at the end of a cul-de-sac. She stared down the block. At nearly every house, families were packing to leave. Sandy shuddered at the thought of all those people, and more, on the roads. In a short time, they would transform from neighbors to motorists in a highway free-for-all.

A few minutes later she saw a pair of headlights coming down the street. It was Mason. He backed the pickup onto the driveway.

Sandy ran to the truck. Mason jumped out and the two of them rushed back to the garage. They were soaked before they got under cover.

"I talked to Ben a few minutes ago. He says they are on their way."

"Hope they hurry. Okay. Move that chair and I'll back the truck into the garage, so we can load everything without getting wet."

Sandy folded the chair and stood aside as Mason backed into the garage. He jumped out and pulled the cover off the truck.

Sandy shook her head, looking at the three big coolers pushed against the cab. "How much stuff did you pack?"

"I got most of our steaks, fifty pounds of ground beef, cheese, and other things that need to be kept cold. It's all packed in ice and taped shut."

"I hope there's room for our bags."

"Not to worry." Mason grabbed one of the bags and threw it aboard. "See? Plenty of room." He rolled the other bag to the truck and put it in.

Mason pulled the cover back over the top of the cargo bay and clicked it down all the way around. "Good to go. What's in the gym bag?"

"I put the billfolds with all the credit cards and the cash from three days of restaurant receipts in here. I also put in our Glock."

Mason looked in the bag. "I'll bet Aaron told you to pack it?"

"He did. Do you think we should take it?"

"You never know what we might run into."

"Yeah, he said we could run into a bunch of out of control people."

"I think he's right. Bring it along."

Sandy closed the bag and threw it into the front seat of the truck. She turned to look down the street for the headlights of their friend's SUV. "I hope Ben and Amy are on the way."

Mason came to stand next to his wife. "Whether they are or not, we can't wait long."

As if to punctuate the moment, Sandy's cell phone rang. "Dad's calling again. He probably wants to know the same thing. How soon are we leaving?" She answered the call. "Hi, Dad, we're packed up and ready to go. Just waiting for our friends."

Aaron's voice in the other end summarized the situation. "I hope they get there soon. Holly is now less than 100 miles from you, churning up the ocean as she goes. It's getting stronger by the minute. The feeder bands must have begun impacting you by now."

"They are. It's raining like hell down here. The palms are bent sideways and the wind ripped the awnings off the house next door."

"It's raining here too, not so hard. I've been checking Highway 27 between here and you. It's still moving well enough. The same isn't true for I-75. Despite having all the lanes running north, it's a mess. Police and national guard are set up along the way with gas, food and medical supplies. I suspect there won't be much security and services on Highway 27. In any case, looters are likely to be shot on sight. You need to be very careful."

"If we drive faster than anyone else, we should be okay."

"For as long as that lasts. Do you have a full tank of gas?"

"We do. I haven't checked with Ben and Amy."

"Who are these people?"

"Amy is Ben's wife. She's pretty rattled. He's a nurse at the hospital. I hope we don't need him."

"I hope so too, but I'm glad to have a medic on hand."

Another set of headlights flashed on the garage. "Someone is coming, Dad. If it's Ben, we will be on the road in a few minutes."

"In that case I won't keep you. Call me back when you're underway." The phone went dead.

Sandy put the cell in her pocket and walked over to join Mason. "Is that them?"

"I think so."

The headlights grew closer until an SUV pulled into the driveway. Ben jumped out, leaning against the wind as he ran into the garage. "Thanks for waiting for us, and giving us a place to go. This storm is one scary mother. Amy is barely holding on."

Mason waved at Amy inside the car. She waved back with little enthusiasm. "It's scary for all of us. I hope you were able to grab some medical supplies."

"I was working in the pharmacy before they cleaned it out. I loaded two boxes of stuff. A little bit of everything."

Mason slapped Ben on the back. "That's good. A little bit of everything is what we need. How much gas do you have?"

"Less than half a tank. I told Amy to fill up today, but she didn't get it done."

"Well, shit. I wouldn't head north to The Villages in normal times with only that much gas. We'll start out, go as far as it lasts. Maybe we'll be lucky and find some gas along the way."

"I'm sorry, Mason. If it helps the hospital paid to have lights and siren installed on my SUV. They said it was for an emergency. I guess this qualifies as that."

Sandy listened while the two talked. "That might give us the edge we need to push around the traffic."

"I think we're gonna need all the edges we can find. Ben's SUV should go first. The two of us should drive the lead car while you and Amy follow us."

Sandy glanced at a distraught Amy in the car. "I think I'll drive."

Ben pulled his coat over his head and rushed through the rain to the SUV. He opened the door and said something to Amy. Sandy couldn't hear what, over the wind, but Ben helped Amy from the car and into the garage. She was crying again.

"Ben told me twice to fill the car with gas. I'm so sorry I didn't. What are we going to do when we run out?"

Mason frowned up at the black, malevolent sky. "We'll cross that bridge when we have to. Until then, Ben and I will drive your car, lights and siren blazing, and hope people get out of our way. You ride in the pickup with Sandy."

"Can't I stay with Ben?"

Sandy hugged Amy. "Then I wouldn't have anyone to talk to."

Lightning flashed with a crash of thunder at the same time.

Mason stared into the clouds. "That was close. We need to get out of here. It's not going to get better. Let's get moving."

Sandy motioned to the pickup. "Hop in, Amy." She turned back to her husband. "How do want to handle this?"

"I'm going to drive like we're in a real emergency vehicle. When people see the lights or hear the siren, they won't realize what we aren't until we've already passed. If we keep moving, I think we'll get most of the way to The Villages before we run out of gas. If there's no gas to be found we'll abandon the SUV and keep going in the pickup."

This possibility seemed like a new development to Amy. "We can't leave our car in the middle of nowhere."

Mason turned to both women. "We can't get stuck out there with only one car. Now listen, Sandy. Stay as close to my bumper as you can. Don't let any other cars slip in between us. The last thing we need is to be separated." Mason paused for a second, then reached into the pickup and grabbed the gym bag. "If we do find some gas, they're gonna want cash. I'll take the bag with the money." He tossed it into the back seat of the SUV.

Sandy held up her phone. "I'll keep my cell plugged in and charging. I think we should stay connected for as long as service lasts."

"I hope it ends up being a three-hour call, and we only hang up when we drive into your Dad's driveway. Anything else?"

The four looked at each other as the thunder rolled. Amy shook her head cheerlessly. Mason walked over to the circuit breaker box and turned off the power. "Let's get the hell outta here."

Chapter 5
Running

Mason slammed the car door. He looked over at Ben. "You okay with me driving?"

"You know the way. I didn't want to say anything in front of Amy, she's already freaked out, but how far will we really get before we run out of gas?

Mason looked at the gas gauge. It was well below half full. "Maybe 150 miles."

"Where will that put us?"

"Someplace close to Winter Haven, I think. That's a better place to look for fuel. It's more built up than other places we'll pass."

"Speaking of that." Mason handed Ben a map. "We might need this."

"I have a GPS in the car."

"If satellite power goes out, we'll need the map. Now, let's get our asses on the road."

"How are we going?"

"I'll take the backstreets to avoid the jams trying to use I-75." Mason jerked the gear shift into reverse and lurched out of the driveway. "We'll use state road 74 across to highway 27 and then straight north to The Villages." He jammed the brakes, shifted into drive, and skidded the first corner. "I hope there isn't a lot of traffic before Highway 27." He glanced in the rear-view mirror to be sure the girls had fallen in behind him. "After that it could get a little dicey."

"Maybe the lights and siren will help."

"I hope to hell they do. If not, we'll be stuck in traffic, burning gas. Traffic laws be damned."

"I hope the girls can keep up."

"Don't worry about that. Sandy will ride my bumper every step of the way."

Ben tuned the radio to the strongest signal he could find. Mason turned up the windshield wipers to high. He switched on the lights and siren.

The howling wind drove the rain in sheets and buffeted the car. Mason gunned the engine and drove faster swerving around traffic. Motorists moved aside for the emergency signals. Some of them honked their horns in anger as they passed and saw it was not a police car or ambulance. Mason tightened his grip on the wheel as he shot past cars making sharp turns winding through town. The heavy rain was flooding low places in the road. It flew in waves as Mason sped through them.

Ben's breath fogged the passenger window as he glanced up a side street through the torrents of rain, prepared to scream a warning if intersecting traffic was bearing down on them. "Clear." He hollered, as Mason raced through the next cross street, and the next, as they worked their way out of town.

Mason gunned past another line of cars. "Once we pass over the highway there won't be as many cars on Route 74."

With the cross streets behind them, Ben switched his view to the front. The flipping wipers were in a losing battle keeping up with the torrents of rain. Cars packed the streets everywhere around them—long, congested lines of cars waiting to pull on the interstate. The flashing lights of emergency vehicles punctuated the commotion. Warning sirens kept nerves on edge.

Mason handed Ben his cell phone. "Call Sandy. We talked about staying connected as long as we could."

❖

"Answer that, Amy. Mason is calling to hook us up. I've got all I can handle keeping up with these guys."

Amy answered the call on the pickup's control screen. Ben's voice spoke to them through the truck speakers. "Hi guys. Mason is busy using both hands to drive, so I'm checking in with you."

"Sandy's busy driving too," groaned Amy. "Does Mason

have to drive so fast? I'm getting thrown all over the pickup."

Mason yelled back "Sorry about that, Amy. I need to drive my wife's gorgeous ass out of town."

Sandy leaned over and spoke into the console speaker. "We need to hang up and call back on Amy's phone. I want to keep my phone open to stay in touch with dad."

The transfer of phones and reestablishment of communications took only a minute. Amy called her husband back. "My phone is plugged into the pickup's power, so we can keep talking."

"Great. You doing okay, honey?"

"I'm scared shitless but it's better now we're moving."

Mason zoomed around another corner and Sandy turned hard to keep up. Amy snatched a handle grip with one hand and steadied the cell phones on the center console with the other.

He shouted from the console. "Route 74 is up ahead. Once we get there, we won't have so many turns. I'm planning on diving around any traffic."

Mason made another sharp turn and onto Route 74. The traffic commanded his full attention. He hugged the center line with his lights flashing and siren blaring as he flew past other cars who moved over enough for the two vehicles to pass.

Sandy followed the SUV as close as she could manage. "If Mason makes a sudden stop, I'll drive right into his backseat."

Amy stared through the windshield. "I'm so scared I can't think."

This is scary for us all."

Sandy's phone rang on the dash screen with a prompt to answer it. She tapped a button. "Hi Dad. What's the latest?"

"Holly hasn't changed course at all. It looks like it will hit Punta Gorda straight on. Right now, she's about ninety miles from landfall. You guys got out just in time."

Sandy looked at the speeding wipers. They were not keeping up with the rainfall, making it hard for her to see any farther than Mason's bumper. "It doesn't feel like we were in time. I can barely see out the windshield for all the rain and the wind is knocking the pickup around. The lights and siren on the other car are helping."

"What lights and siren?"

"The hospital where Ben's a nurse, installed them on his car."

"That makes me feel a whole lot better. Are they working?"

"Yeah. Mason is using them to zip around cars. Yikes. Hang on." She swerved the wheel to the right, following Mason into a spot in the traffic. A pair of emergency vehicles roared past going the other way. She swerved back to the left as Mason pulled out of the line of cars and back to straddling the center line. He sped up. Sandy jammed the accelerator to keep up. "Sorry about that. I had to follow Mason."

"It's okay. How's Ben's wife?"

Sandy looked across at Amy. "Hey, you okay?"

Amy nodded—barely—and stared straight ahead. Sandy thought she was staring at nothing.

"It's been a hard day and night for all of us."

"I'm sure. I thought something was wrong when I heard your friend screaming."

Sandy shook her head. She didn't remember Amy screaming. Was she as disjointed as her? Aaron's voice sounded soothing. "I hadn't intended this call to last even this long but can you stand a little more?"

"Sure. Shoot."

"Where are you, about, now?"

"East of Punta Gorda, on State road 74. The traffic is heavy and slow moving. I can't imagine what it will be like when we hit 27."

"No better, that's for sure. How's your gas situation?"

"We have plenty but Ben and Amy's SUV had less than half a tank when we left. We'll drive as far as we can and hope to find some gas somewhere."

There was a pause before Aaron continued. "Having to stop and hunt for gas will slow you down. It could also be very dangerous. You might be better off to abandon the SUV and double up in the pickup."

"That's what Mason said. He's driving the SUV. We'll go as far as we can before we make that decision."

"That's right. Take it one step at a time."

"What are you hearing about the power staying on?

"All sorts of advice on what to do if it goes out. I think that means it will. I've hooked my generator up to the breaker box, so I can open the switch if we do lose power."

"I hope our cells keep running."

"Cell towers these days have back-up power sources. I don't think they're a problem unless the wind takes them down, or they get flooded."

"I didn't know that. Anything else?"

"Plenty for now. Stay in touch the best you can."

Sandy looked away from the console and at her friend. "Hear that, Amy? A friendly voice all the way to The Villages."

The terrified woman shrugged her shoulders and hugged herself around her stomach. "We gotta get there first."

Aaron laid his phone down and turned to Angie. He spread out his hands and shrugged in a feeble gesture. "I've never felt so helpless."

"Well, stop it. We have every reason to believe they'll get here safe."

"I hope so. Wonder what they'll do when they run out of gas?"

"Sandy said it. They'll decide when they have to. Until then, we swallow our worry and wait."

"Isn't it in the marriage manual that it's the wife who does all the dithering?"

"This is your week to be the shrinking violet."

Aaron waved his hand with good-natured humor. "What have we got to nibble on?"

"Nibbles coming up." Angie angled off to the kitchen.

When she left, Aaron turned the sound back up on the Weather Channel. The models were changing so fast the forecasters contradicted themselves with new updates. The picture was grim. Even at this late hour, Evan Driscoll still commanded the center chair and reported.

These two storms are now approximately six hundred miles from each other. That is well within their mutual storm coverage, and we are seeing significant interaction between them.

This is known as the Fujiwara Effect. In the past, two results come from hurricanes near one another. One outcome is the larger storm absorbs the smaller one. Or, they circle each other and spin off in different directions. We may be seeing this phenomenon now. Both hurricanes are beginning to dance around each other and their storm tracks are no longer even remotely predictable. This makes the job of forecasting the immediate future of both Karl and Holly a nightmare for meteorologists.

Here is what we know now. Karl has begun to track more to the south. It will still make landfall along the Space Coast, but has increased its speed and will come ashore at least twelve hours sooner than earlier predicted. It has not lost any of its intensity and is still a very dangerous Category 5 hurricane.

Holly is likewise still Cat 5 in intensity. It is now eighty-five miles south and west of Punta Gorda. If anything, Holly is more intense and life-threatening than Karl. Barometric pressure is down to an almost record low at 900 millibars. It's still tracking north but interaction with Karl is causing it to spin more to the east.

As mandatory evacuations continue, on both the east and west coasts of Florida, areas inland which previously were under hurricane advisories are now updated to warnings. This includes metropolitan Orlando, Tampa, an all central Florida.

Angie came back to the office with a plate of cookies. "What's Evan saying now?"

"He's beginning to talk about the Fujiwara Effect of two hurricanes colliding. So far, he's staying with the common knowledge of what happens when they do. He knows the idea of two hurricanes combining into one super storm is not the way it works. However, all previous data is based on hurricanes combining over water. Nobody has the slightest idea of what will happen if they come together over land."

"Do you?"

"Only guesses. For sure there would be destructive high winds and a tremendous amount of rain. Neither of which would be good for us."

"Sandy and Mason must be going through exactly that trying to drive up here."

"I'm sure that's so. I haven't said anything to Sandy, other than tell her to hurry. No need to add more stress while they're driving through this monstrous freak of nature."

Angie eased onto the couch. "Lord, help them. Bring my girl home safe."

Chapter 6
The Road to Hell

<u>Early Tuesday morning</u>
Ben shined a flashlight on the map. He looked over at Mason. "Are you going to take this other state road going north off Route 74 to intersect with Highway 27?"

"I was going to, but I'm worried about gas. We can't afford to run out in the middle of nowhere." Mason glanced at Ben. "Now, don't go off on Amy again because we have fuel problems."

"It wouldn't be a problem if she had gotten some gas."

"She said the lines were long. Maybe most of the stations had run out."

"Not much good now."

"That other route might not be such a great idea anyway. It's a smaller road than this one."

Mason swung far onto the shoulder of the left lane to pass a line of cars. He kept talking. "Right now, I'm worried about what's ahead on the main highway. We need to go as far as we can. That's when the lights and sirens will matter the most."

The last thirty miles on Route 74 got more congested by the minute. Mason drove around lines of traffic and a couple accidents using the left shoulder of the road. So far, they hadn't seen anymore emergency vehicles. Sandy kept the pickup neatly tucked in behind the SUV.

The closer to Highway 27 they got, the more traffic they encountered. State patrol cars lights were flashing when they reached the intersection,

Mason peered through the windshield. The wipers giving scant relief from the pelting rain. Highway patrolmen, with strong hand lights, were directing traffic amid the downpour and growing wind. Cars from Route 74 flowed into the heavier lines on Highway 27. "This is where we find out how much our lights and siren help."

Ben looked around. "I think the power is out."

It was eerie. The street lights, traffic signals, illuminated signs on businesses were all dark. Only the flashing lights of emergency vehicles shone through the driving rain.

A patrolman, coat and pants whipping in the wind, signaled them into an open lane where another patrolman checked vehicles as they passed. That section of the road ahead looked almost clear. Mason slowed and cracked his window as they reached the checkpoint. "Medical emergency."

The officer looked in the car and across to Ben, still wearing his nurses' scrubs, and waved them through. Mason gunned the engine. Sandy didn't hesitate either. She followed her husband close behind before anyone could object.

Mason leaned forward to get a better view. "See what they're doing? They've turned the southbound lanes into additional lanes headed north, and left the outside lane for emergency vehicles. It's working. If we can stay in this lane, we should make good time."

"That cop didn't even ask a question."

"His job is to keep traffic moving, not make judgement calls. We'll drive flat out until we run out of gas. Start looking for a station with lights still on."

"How could there be any lights with the power off?"

"Backup generators could make enough power to run a couple of pumps. A few stations might still be operating."

"Why would they?"

"They probably thought being so far inland, Holly wouldn't be as big a threat. Some stations might try to stay open hoping to make a fast buck from people willing to pay anything to get some gas."

"Like us?"

"Exactly, keep your eyes open." Mason picked up the cell. "You still with us, honey?"

"Still here." Sandy's voice came from the phone. "Speak up,

I can't hear you very well through the wind and rain. With all the power out, I can barely see where I'm going."

"I told Ben to look for any gas stations with lights on. You do the same. Have Amy focus her attention on that."

"I'll tell her. She needs something to do."

Amy wrung her hands together in her lap. Sandy hoped it was calming her. It didn't look like it was doing much good.

Amy stared out the window. "All I can see are the headlights of other cars. There's no power on the streets or buildings. It's so dark."

"Mason says there might be a few gas stations open. You need to keep a sharp eye."

"How can I see anything through this storm?"

"That's why we need to keep looking. Mason and I are busy trying to stay on the road. You and Ben will spot something sooner. Can you do that for us?"

"I'll try."

"Listen, we may not have many chances. You have to do more than try."

"I'm so scared I can't concentrate."

"We're all scared. We're in this together. That includes you, lady. Now wipe your damn eyes and help me out. We gotta keep moving. Everything will be better when we get to my mom and dad's place but that's still a long way from here, and we need gas before then. If you spot a lighted station, sing out loud and clear."

Amy wiped more tears from her eyes. "Okay."

There was nothing more Sandy could say. She had to hope Amy got the message. At least she was now staring through the windshield like she was looking for something.

Mason drove on. "Turn up the radio. Let's see if they're saying anything about traffic on this road."

Ben cranked up the volume and the two listened for a few

minutes. The coverage centered on conditions on I-75. Even with traffic using all the lanes on the freeway for northbound evacuees, the announcer said the road was jammed with slow-moving cars.

Ben sat back in his seat. "I'm sure glad we didn't try going that way. What's going to happen when Holly hits the coast?"

"That depends on where people are when it does. The interstate is so close to the coast in some places south of Tampa, it'll flood. People caught in that are in big trouble."

"I can't even imagine what that'll be like." Ben leaned forward and stared out the windshield. "It's raining buckets, and we're getting knocked around by the wind."

"I saw dust storms as bad as this in Afghanistan."

"You did? What did you do?"

"Mostly we looked for cover to ride out the storms. Too bad we don't have that option here. No choice but keep moving."

Mason emphasized that by swerving onto the shoulder of the road to pass a multi-car accident. He added a hoot on the siren as he passed by.

"I didn't know you served in the Middle-East. What did you do?"

"Long-range coverage of unit operations. I was the sniper."

"See much action?"

"More than I want to remember."

"I'll bet this seems like nothing much?"

"Are you kidding? Life-threatening situations are always life-threatening. This storm is like an ugly enemy who never stops shooting at you, and you can't shoot back. You take a deep breath and forget how scared you are. I'm trying to stay on the road."

"I thought I was the only one about to crap his pants."

"Yeah, well if you need another reason, take a look at the gas gauge."

Ben leaned over and looked at the instrument panel. The line on the gauge now showed less than a quarter tank of gas. "How much farther do you think we'll get?"

"Maybe fifty miles if we were driving on a sunny day. I'm going faster than the rest of the traffic but it's still a crawl. We should think in terms of time, not gallons."

"Okay. How much time?"

"No more than an hour. The odds of finding a place to fill up are a long shot. We need to start thinking of dumping this car and cramming everyone into the pickup. I don't think that's such a bad thing. It's simpler and safer."

The roar of the wind made conversation difficult. Ben sat back in the seat. There was not much else to say.

An hour later, Mason looked at the gas gauge for the twentieth time. "If we don't find something in the next few minutes, we'll have to pull over, empty the SUV and keep going in the pickup."

The blare of the horn from the pickup made Mason look over his shoulder. The high beams on the pickup flashed. Mason slowed and peered through the windshield. He had not seen it before, but lights flickered on a single pump at a gas station ahead. He made a quick turn to the left, onto a frontage road, and saw a hand-painted sign stuck near the entrance. *Gas. Cash only.*

Mason reached into the back seat and grabbed the gym bag with the cash from the restaurant. He put it on the console between him and Ben. Reaching into the bag, Mason pulled out the Glock, chambered a round, and shoved it into the space between the seat and the door. Then he pulled up and stopped. A bearded man ran out of the service office. He had a shotgun tucked under his arm.

Mason rolled down the window. "Can we buy some gas?"

The bearded man looked darkly at him. "Fifty bucks a gallon."

Mason didn't want to start an argument. "Fill 'er up."

"What about your truck?"

"It doesn't need gas."

"I'll take the cash first."

The bearded man watched Mason rummage in the gym bag, grab a handful of bills, and stick his fist out the window.

The man's eyes grew wide when he saw the piles of cash. "Looks like you got lots of money."

"Can we have the gas now?"

"Sure. Hand over that bag." The man took a half step back and took the shotgun in both hands.

"Charging fifty bucks a gallon for gas is bad enough. When this is all over, people will remember what you did."

"Not me, mister. The owner took off hours ago. Left me to look after things. I hooked up the generator and went into business for myself. I've made a bundle tonight."

Mason stared into the man's eyes and handed the money out the window. "Fine. Here's more for your bundle. Pump the gas."

"I said I wanted your bag."

"Don't ask for more than you can handle."

The man backed up another step and pointed the shotgun at Mason. "You're the one with more than you can handle. Gimme that bag." He pumped a round into the chamber and pulled the trigger. The blast blew away part of the driver's door. Mason winced in pain.

"The next round goes right in your face, asshole. Now hand over that bag."

Mason didn't think. He reached down and fumbled for the Glock in the debris of the door. His fingers felt the cold steel fill his hand. With a jerk he pulled it up to the window.

The bearded man yelled as he pumped another round into the chamber. He never had a chance to pull the trigger. Mason shot him in the chest twice. The man went down in a heap.

Ben opened his door and jumped out of the SUV. "What the hell, Mason." He ran around the car and knelt next to the man lying in a pool of blood. Mason got out as well.

Sandy and Amy got out of the pickup and ran up to the

two.

Amy put her hand to her mouth and screamed uncontrollably. Then she gasped. "Aahh, what have you done? You awful man. Why did you do that?"

Sandy slapped Amy so hard she staggered from the blow. Then Sandy gathered Amy in her arms and hugged as she stared at the scene.

Ben shook his head. "He's dead. What do we do now?"

As he spoke, another car pulled into the station.

Mason looked at it over his shoulder. "We get the hell out of here. Everybody back inside, we're leaving."

Sandy took Amy by the arm and dragged her back to the pickup. Mason pulled Ben off the ground and pushed him toward the passenger door. "Come on, Ben. Get in the car."

Mason's face grimaced in pain as he slid into the SUV and drove off, out from beneath the roof over the pumps and back into the rain. Sandy slammed her door and followed Mason.

Amy was sobbing again.

Mason turned the lights and siren on and angled his way through the congested cars. He careened through an open intersection and back into the emergency lane. He raced the engine, clipping the front of a car in his way. The SUV rocked violently. When he glanced into the rear-view mirror, Sandy was following him close behind.

Ben stared at Mason. "I thought I was going to die when that guy blew a hole in the side."

"You would have if I didn't have the gun."

"It happened so fast."

"Yeah, that's always the way it is."

"You killed a man because of a few gallons of gas."

The strain of the last hours, plus the grisly scene at the gas station, reached overload for Mason. "For Christ's sake, stop it. I killed him because he was about to kill me, us, and steal our money. We still don't have any gas and I don't think we're going to find any. We'll drive till we run out and then go on together in the pickup."

Ben put his head down. "I'm supposed to save lives, not watch people die. Will this nightmare never end?"

Chapter 7
Struggling for Safety

Mason's white knuckles gripped the steering wheel. The traffic kept him from thinking back to his killing a man at the gas station. The rain and wind blurred his vision, but not the image in his head of the station attendant, shotgun in hand, lying dead in the mud and the blood and the gore. He still felt sick at what he had done.

Thought that was behind me. Guess not.

His thigh and butt throbbed from the buckshot and shrapnel. He'd put his hand down his pants at the station and felt the damage. It was mostly flesh wounds. The bleeding was slowing faster than the pain. It hurt like hell.

Ben looked at Mason from across the car. "You okay?" When Mason didn't answer Ben leaned closer, grasped Mason's bicep, and raised his voice. "Are you okay?"

"Hold the wheel for me."

Mason rolled down the window. Ben grabbed the wheel and Mason vomited violently. He had a strong stomach and most of it went out of the car.

He wiped his mouth on his shirt, took the wheel from Ben and stared straight ahead. "Thanks, I got it."

"I can't believe what happened. That guy must have been nuts?"

"Whatever. It cost him his life."

"Why didn't you give him the bag of money?"

"I should have never let the boy see it. When we drove up, I figured a shakedown. I was willing to hand over the cash, get the gas, and be on our way. When he saw the money, he got greedy and stopped thinking. If I hadn't done what I did, we'd be dead, all of us."

"You pulled your gun and shot him so fast. I wasn't thinking either."

"It wasn't think time, it was do time."

"It was horrible, that's what it was."

"Let's hope we get to The Villages before something else happens."

Ben sat back in the seat and said nothing for several minutes.

Mason felt Ben staring at him and glanced over. "Want to say something?"

"I'm glad I don't have to live with what you did. But I think you did the right thing."

Sandy knew her husband did the right thing too. He never talked about his experiences in combat, and she had not pressed him for details. Now his training forced him to take an action she was sure he didn't want, but was ready to do. Was she grateful he'd killed a man? Of course not, but if he hadn't, she and Amy would be dead. No question in her mind. There was no time to think about that now. It was all she could do to stay tucked in behind the speeding SUV.

She jumped when her father's voice came from the speaker grille. "Sandy, are you still there?"

"I'm here, Dad."

"What's happening? Did you get gas?"

"No, we didn't. I can't talk about it now. We're back on the road. Mason will drive the SUV until it's empty, and then we'll keep going in the pickup."

Angie came on the phone. "Your voice is shaking, Sandy. Are you okay?"

"Hi, Mom. All of us are still in one piece, but the last hour is something I want to forget."

"You can tell me when I see you. Do you know where you are?"

"I haven't seen much else but Mason's bumper. All I know is how many miles we've driven."

Aaron joined in. "How many miles?"

Sandy looked at the odometer and figured in her head. "About 120 miles."

"Any chance of finding some gas?"

"I don't think Mason will stop again until we have to."

"Whatever happened won't change the fact you'll run out of gas in minutes. You need to be ready for that."

Sandy didn't answer. Something crashed heavily into the side of the pickup jolting both her and Amy. The truck swerved left. She yanked the steering wheel trying to regain control. The vehicle lunged back to the right. Sandy looked in the side mirror. A car had T-boned the pickup, hitting near the left, rear tire and crushing the side. She saw pieces of both cars fall away as the truck pulled ahead. The sharp grinding sound told her the side panel had collapsed and was chewing the tire to pieces.

Sandy yelled into the phone. "Mason, a car hit us from the side. I never saw it. The back fender is scrapping the tire. We have to stop."

Mason screamed. "Are you okay?"

"Yeah. Rattled to our bones."

"I'm gonna pull off up here. Stay close behind."

The flashing lights of the SUV veered to the left. Sandy forced the pickup to follow. Straight ahead she barely made out the outline of a deserted gas station. Mason drove the SUV under one of the big canopies over the pumps and stopped. Sandy slammed to a stop behind. Rain blew horizontally under the canopy, the wind howled.

Mason steadied himself along the hood of the SUV as he limped to the pickup. Sandy rolled down the window.

"Are you really alright?"

"I'm okay. Look at the damage."

Mason braced against the wind and walked to the back of

the truck. He pulled at the crumpled fender and shone a flashlight on the mess. Then he went back to Sandy.

"The tire's shot. The fender and the side of the pickup are fucked. If I put on the spare, it'll get shredded."

"Terrific. What do we do now?"

Mason laced his hands behind his head. "We'll leave the truck and go on in the SUV."

"It's out of gas."

"Not for long."

Mason hobbled around to the other side of the truck and unsnapped the bed cover. The wind carried it away. He pushed one of the smashed coolers out of the way, opened his toolbox and removed a coiled rubber tube. He grabbed it and came back around the truck to Sandy.

"Pull the truck on the other side so the gas tanks line up. I'm going to siphon the gas in the truck into the SUV. While I'm doing that, help Ben put our bags in their car."

"I have to move Amy too."

"Something I don't know?"

"Nah. I'm kidding. She's not doing much to help. She's so freaked out, she can't think."

"Shit. I can't think."

"Well enough to keep us from getting blown away by that nut job at the gas station."

"I was only reacting. Didn't have a choice."

"I know. Maybe Ben does too. Amy is out of it."

"Has she said anything?"

"Not much about that or anything else. Maybe she thinks you killed a man for no reason."

"No time for that now. Get her into the SUV."

"That may be all she can handle right now."

Sandy backed the SUV next to side of the pickup. Mason fed one end of the tube into the pickup and sucked on the tube. He choked when the gas started, spitting it out wildly.

While the gas drained, Mason looked around in the rear seat of the truck and grabbed a semi-clean towel. He shoved it down his pants to soak up the blood. Scraping the towel across the jagged wounds made him stagger in pain. He took a deep breath and focused on the siphon. He didn't want the others to know about his wounds.

Sandy helped Ben take the bags from the bed of the pickup and throw them into the SUV. She went back to the pickup, opened the door and touched Amy "Come on. We're switching cars."

Amy didn't move. "I'm not getting in a car with that murderer."

"He's no murderer, and yes you are."

"Aahh." Amy jerked her shoulders. "Get your hands off me."

Ben came up next to Sandy. "Amy, you gotta move. We have to go."

"No."

He put his hand on his wife's shoulder and leaned in to look directly into her face. She stared ahead as if he was not there.

He went back to the SUV, opened his medical bag and pulled out a syringe and a small bottle. He filled it and went back to the pickup. The wind blowing his hair straight back. "This will settle you down."

Amy glared at her husband. "I don't want any of that. Leave me alone."

Sandy pinned Amy's shoulders to the seat while Ben injected the drug. Her head lolled toward Ben, then her body slumped. Ben held Amy upright while Sandy guided her toward the back seat of the SUV. Ben jumped in next to her.

The siphon finished. Mason threw the hose back into his toolbox and hefted it into the back of the SUV, slamming the hatch shut. He gingerly moved around to the driver's side and slid into the seat. He started the engine and checked the tank. It now showed over half a tankful.

Sandy got in the front seat and looked around the car. Ben looked calm enough. Amy's eyes were glassy. She patted her husband on the knee. "Let's get out of here."

As she spoke, a gust of wind swirled under the station canopy ripping it from its foundation. Mason gunned the engine and shot out from under the falling debris. As he drove away, the canopy collapsed. A heavy thud smashed the pickup, covering it with rubble.

Sandy looked over her shoulder. "That was close. Everything is trying to kill us."

Mason said nothing, blinked away the pain, and maneuvered the vehicle back into the lanes of cars. The lights and siren pierced the night.

Sandy stared through the wet windshield. "Where are we?"

"Past Winter Haven, I think. We still have sixty or so miles to go. At least I can stop worrying about gas."

"And we still have the lights and siren."

"With this heavy rain, people can't see very far, but they'll see the lights and hear us coming."

"I'm gonna call Dad back. I lost him when we wrecked the pickup."

Sandy punched the number and kept punching it with each 'out of service' or 'lines busy' signal. She got through on the twentieth try.

The sound of tension was clear in her father's voice. "We've called and called. Are you all right?"

"Still in one piece, but it hasn't been easy."

Sandy went on to tell Aaron about the accident and the change of vehicles.

"Sounds like you've been lucky. I'm glad you still have the lights and siren. Can you tell me where you are?"

"Mason says we're north of Winter Haven with another

sixty miles to go. It's not raining so much, but the congestion is getting worse."

"One thing at a time. Karl is nearing landfall on the Space Coast. The worst of Holly is south of you. There's a little hole in th..."

Crackle, pop, skeezzik.

"Wad you say? You cut out."

"I said you're in a little open space. For the next few hours, the rain will let up on you a bit."

"I guess I ought to breathe a little easier, but, Dad, what we've gone through tonight is so terrible, I can't think straight. And we aren't there yet."

"I'm hoping to help you out on that. I've been looking at the map and I think there's a way to get you out of the main traffic flow."

Mason was listening. "Tell me what you have in mind."

"I've been monitoring traffic on Highway 27. The congestion gets heavier as you get closer to the turnp..."

Scree, Beep-beep-beep.

"Say again. You cut out."

"The turnpike is completely jammed and at a standstill. You should take smaller roads. That'll get you around that mess. Is your GPS still working?"

"For now."

"Okay. Turn off on State Road 474. It's about ten miles beyond I-4."

Mason pointed at the dash display and Sandy pulled up a larger scale on the map. He looked where she pointed. "I see it."

"That road will take you to Highway 33." Aaron went on. "After it passes over the turnpike, it ought to be easier to manage the rest of the way."

Mason nodded his head as if Aaron could see him. "We'll be on the lookout for the turn."

"You guys hold on a little longer. Angie will cook you

breakfast."

"Sounds good."

Sandy patted his shoulder. "You keep your eyes on the road, darling. I'll keep watching for the turnoff."

"Thanks, honey." Mason shouted over his shoulder to Ben. "How's Amy doing?

"She's dopey, but quiet for now. I'll look for the turnoff too."

A half hour later they almost missed the sign to the state road because the wind had blown it to a crazy angle. Mason pulled off the main highway. A tree had fallen, partly on the smaller road, and he had to make a wide turn to get around it. The rear wheels sunk into the sand on the shoulder. The SUV twisted and almost ground to a stop. Mason gave it the gas, and they slid back onto the pavement. The rain made it hard to see more than a few yards.

Aaron was right about there being less traffic on this smaller road. Mason was able to relax a bit. It didn't last long. Minutes later a panicky deer jumped onto the road in front of the SUV. Mason swerved but clipped the rear of the deer with the front, right fender. It knocked the deer down but Mason lost track of it in the rain.

Hope I didn't kill something else today.

There was still traffic on this road, but much less than before. Mason maneuvered to the next intersection and made the turn onto Highway 33.

After that, it took only patience to finish the drive. Before long, the familiar streets of The Villages began passing by.

A sudden lull in the wind made it eerie. Silent. The wind died like the gas attendant, only the wind had no blood. Two more turns. Sandy let out a long collective sigh of relief as they turned onto the driveway of her Dad's home.

This must be how Dorothy felt when she and Toto got back to Kansas. There's no place like home.

Chapter 8
Home, Not So Sweet, Home

<u>Four a.m. Tuesday morning</u>

Aaron's stomach was sour. His muscles ached from staying up all night. He wished he could take a nap, but his daughter Sandy, son-in-law, Mason, and the other couple were only a few blocks away. He stared out his front window. The rain shortened his distance vision. The relentless wind whipped the big Sylvester palm in his front yard. It looked like a dog shaking its head to shed the water.

Angie came into the office. "If you're gonna run out in the rain to help everyone inside, put on your coveralls." She tossed them to him.

"Thanks." He stepped into the coveralls and zipped it up over his shorts and T-shirt. "The perfect wet suit for a hurricane."

"Don't forget to pull up the hood and tie it down."

As she spoke, the SUV pulled into the driveway. Aaron saw it and ran out, leaning into the wind. "Stay here. We'll be right back."

Sandy opened her door and stepped out into her father's arms. "Oh, Daddy, I'm so happy to be here."

"So glad you're safe. We prayed you'd get here in one piece. Let's get you guys inside and out of this weather."

On the other side of the car, Mason was weakly easing himself out the other door and leaning against the car. The wind tore the door from his hand and slammed it shut.

Aaron saw him struggling and came around the car. He looked at the face of his son-in-law. Mason was pale. His eyes had a distant, detached, look. His fingers still curled from fighting the steering wheel. His lips were locked.

Aaron saw pain written on his face. "Come on, Pal, you're getting wet. How bad are you hurt?"

"Not terrible, but I sure need something for the pain."

Sandy yelled over the top of the SUV. "Go on in. Ben and I have Amy."

Mason and Aaron headed for the front door. Ben and Sandy followed with Amy between them. Her arms draped over their shoulders to keep her from wobbling as they guided her along. Aaron steadied Mason.

Angie held the door open as everyone scrambled into the house. She passed out dry towels. Aaron gave her a, there's-something-else-going-on, look as he supported Mason. Angie tilted her head toward the guest bedroom. Aaron stayed with Mason until they got into the bedroom where his knees buckled.

Aaron caught him. "Let's get you on the bed."

Mason eased onto his good side exposing his shredded jeans.

"My God, man. What on earth happened? You look like you've been shot."

"Can you get Ben in here?"

Aaron rushed down the hall to the living room. Sandy and Ben were helping Amy get comfortable on the couch.

Angie jumped at his arrival. "Everything okay in there?"

"We need some medical help."

Ben turned. "What for?"

Aaron put out his hand. "You must be Ben. Glad to meet you. We'll get acquainted later. Right now, I need you in the bedroom."

Sandy turned to face her father. "What's wrong?"

"Don't know yet. I need Ben to take a look. Come with me."

Aaron put his arm around Sandy as they followed Ben to the bedroom. When they came in, Aaron saw Mason hadn't moved.

Ben's eyes narrowed when he saw Mason's bloody pants. "I wondered how that shotgun blast could have missed you. I guess it didn't. Let's get your jeans off, so I can see." Ben headed for the door, his voice trailing over his shoulder. "Hang in there a second while I get my bag." Aaron took off Mason's shoes. "This will make it easier."

Mason nodded and clenched his jaw. "Thanks."

A wet Ben came back to the room. Water dripped from his clothing. "I had to run out to the car to get my bag. Yea Gads, is it coming down out there." He opened his bag and pulled out a pair of scissors. "I'm gonna cut off your jeans."

The scissors neatly sliced the material. Aaron helped Ben pull the pieces away. Mason's underwear was torn and bloody. Ben cut and removed them. He leaned down, staring closely at the wounds.

Aaron stared too. "That's awful."

Mason grimaced. "I can imagine." He rolled to face Ben. "Can you give me something for the pain before you start."

Ben didn't answer. He reached into his bag and made up a syringe. He turned back to Mason. "This will stop the pain and knock you out for a while. Long enough for me to do what I have to do." He injected the drug.

Aaron eased Mason back until he was lying face down on the bed, welcome relief on his eyes.

Sandy blinked in horror at her husband's torn and still bleeding flesh. She put her hands to her face and then knelt next to the bed. She put her arms around his shoulders. "Mason, I'm so sorry."

"Gonna be alright," slurred Mason.

Ben put a hand on both Aaron and Sandy. "I need room to work. You guys are in the way, and I don't need anybody looking over my shoulder. I can handle this. Wait outside. I'll call you when I'm done."

"Come on, honey, let Ben do what he can. I'll fix you something to drink." Aaron pushed Sandy out of the room and closed the door.

Angie was waiting for them in the hall. Sandy fell into her mother's arms. Angie focused sharply on Aaron. "Is somebody going to tell me what's going on?"

"Mason has wounds from a shotgun. Ben is working on him. That's all I know."

"You didn't ask?"

"I didn't have a chance. Ben sent us out. Can we go to the living room? I'm gonna fix Sandy a drink. You want one?"

Angie nodded and led Sandy away. Aaron went to the kitchen, opened a cabinet and pulled out a bottle of brandy. He put ice in a couple of glasses, then got another glass for himself. He poured three generous drinks and took two of them to the living room. Sandy and Angie took the glasses, and they both took a healthy gulp. Aaron went back into the kitchen for his drink. As he picked up his glass, he took a deep breath.

Gotta keep it together.

He returned to the living room and sat down. "Can you tell me what happened?"

Sandy took another swallow. "We found a gas station still open. When we pulled in, there was a guy by the pumps with a shotgun. I couldn't hear what was going on but Mason tried to give him some money. Then the guy backed up and shot the car. He pointed the shotgun at Mason screaming something. Mason pulled out the Glock and shot him. After he and Ben jumped out of the car, Amy and I got out too. Ben told us the guy was dead. I took his word for it. I couldn't even look. It was terrible. Then another car pulled in behind us. Mason said to get back in the cars. We did and drove off."

Aaron sat back in his chair. His warning for Sandy to be prepared for anything ended up dwarfed by actual events. He couldn't say he was surprised. It didn't explain the woman slumping on his couch. "What about your friend?"

"Amy had trouble dealing with this from the start. Running away from the storm was bad enough. The fireworks at the gas station made it worse. Then we got clobbered and wrecked the pickup. We had to jam into one car. It pushed her over the edge.

She started screaming and wouldn't get out of the pickup. Ben gave her a shot of something."

Amy stirred from the couch and muttered. "He murdered that man."

Aaron pressed his lips together and shook his head. "I see what you mean. I don't know how any of you managed to keep going."

"I almost didn't."

"Mason never told you he was hurt?"

"Not a word, Dad. I didn't know anything until I saw him with his pants cut away ... how bad it was."

This was too much for Angie. She set her glass onto the coffee table. "Somebody better tell me how bad he's hurt."

Aaron shrugged. "I've no idea. He's got a bunch of holes in his butt and leg. It sure looked like a mess. I got the impression Ben could handle it."

Amy went on mumbling. Aaron stared at the wall trying to think straight. Twenty minutes ago, he was only thinking of the big storms closing in around him. Now he had a good deal more to consider. He was glad Angie changed the subject.

"You must be hungry. What can I fix you?"

"I'm famished, Mom. Can I have a sandwich or something? Make something for Amy too."

Angie finished off her drink and stood up. She called over her shoulder as she headed to the kitchen. "Coming right up."

Aaron turned to Sandy. "I knew something had happened, but then you had that accident and I got busy figuring out the best way to get you here. Since I didn't know what happened before, or that Mason was hurt, I concentrated on that."

"So, did I. I was sitting right next to him, and he never let on he was injured."

"Pretty brave on his part. He must have blocked the pain to stay focused on the road and not add any more tension to your situation. I gotta tell you, when he got in the house, there was nothing left. I had to help him lay down. The pain overwhelmed him."

"I want to go in there. I guess I can't. Oh, Daddy, everything's jumbled."

Think. You've got four terrified people. Keep it together.

Aaron sat down next to her, closed his eyes tight and took his daughter in his arms. "Everything is going to be okay."

"As if you knew." She smirked at her father. "I still believe you."

Aaron laughed. It seemed such a hollow sound in this dark world. But it made him feel better. "Ha. There you are. A comfy house, food to eat and a stiff drink. What could be more perfect?"

Angie popped out of the kitchen with a tray of sandwiches and glasses. "I heard that. Not to be a mood-wrecker, but have you thought about what to do when this house becomes not so comfy?"

"Later. We have some time. For now, let's pay attention to what's right in front of us."

Aaron winced at Sandy's face, the concern for Mason smeared across it as she looked at her mother. "Ben is taking so long."

Angie put the tray down. "He'll be done when he's done." She handed Sandy a sandwich on a plate.

Aaron got up and walked to the couch. He leaned in to Amy. "How about you, young lady, you must be hungry?" He took another plate off the tray and sat it in front of her.

Amy looked at Aaron, then the plate. She shook her head a little. Aaron could see she was trying to clear her mind. He picked up the plate and handed it to her. She took a sandwich and nibbled it.

"There you go. Food will make you feel better." There was little joy in Amy's grimace, but she took another bite.

"We haven't been introduced. I'm Sandy's dad. My name is Aaron. This is my wife Angie. We're glad you made it here safely."

Amy gave him a curious smile, like he was the only sane man in the world. "Thank you. I've never been through a night like this. The shot my husband gave me made it feel like I was dreaming. I'm better now. A lot better since we're here."

Aaron tried not to show his relief when Angie slipped onto the coach next to Amy. "It's okay, honey." She put her hand softly on Amy's arm. "You're safe now."

The two began talking. Aaron sat back down, staring helplessly at his feet. Angie was always better at the soft stuff than him.

Sandy jumped up. "I can't stand it. I'm looking in to see how Mason is."

Aaron looked at her with a level stare. "Better knock first."

She was part way to the hall when Ben came out, drying his hands on a towel. Everyone got up and joined Sandy.

With the ease of experience, Ben's arms went out in expressive relief. "Mason's going to be fine. He's gonna have a real sore butt for a while. I took a dozen shotgun pellets and pieces of metal out of him. I bandaged him up, started an IV, gave him a big dose of antibiotics and another shot for pain. He'll sleep for a while."

Aaron went over and shook Ben's hand. "Thanks a lot. We're grateful for the help."

Sandy kissed Ben's cheek. "Thanks, Ben. You're a good friend. Can I peek in on Mason?"

"Sure."

Sandy hurried off.

"I fixed sandwiches. Would you like one?"

"That would be nice, Mrs. Colson."

"My goodness, call me Angie, please."

"Could you also fix a cup of coffee?"

"I'll start a new pot right now."

Aaron waved Ben to the couch and then excused himself to get something from his office. He needed a quiet moment to think. The last two days had scrapped Aaron's mind raw. The previous minutes made it bleed.

As bad as the drive must have been, what faced them now could be worse. Choices made; plans considered. He had to turn the others away from the tragedy on the road and start them thinking about the catastrophe that lay ahead.

Sandy stepped from the bedroom as Aaron came back from the office. Sandy plopped down on the couch and looked at her father.

Aaron took a seat on the coffee table, facing the others. "Getting here was only the start. In the next hours these two hurricanes are going to hit us straight on. We gotta be ready."

Sandy poked at the chips on her plate. "What's the latest on these storms?"

"I haven't kept up for the last few hours. For sure, it's not getting better."

The telephone rang. Aaron glanced with annoyance at the muted TV screen. The caller ID said it was Evan Driscoll at the Weather Channel.

"Ah shit. Gimme a minute."

Chapter 9
Dark Forecasts

Aaron snatched the telephone. "What?"

"Hi Aaron. Sorry about the call. Are you guys okay down there?"

"Our daughter and her husband are here after the drive from Punta Gorda. He was injured trying to buy some gas. Another couple came with them. One of them is a nurse. He worked on Mason, and he's gonna be all right. Other than that, we're doing peachy."

"Not for long, I'm afraid. I'm sorry about your troubles. Have you paid been tracking the storms?"

"Not lately, Evan. Tell me what's going on."

"Holly made a direct hit on Punta Gorda. It increased in strength to a Cat 5 plus. The eye wall winds are over 180 miles an hour. The pressure is down to a record low at 890 millibars. I don't think there's much left of the town. The storm is now moving up the coast causing catastrophic damage. Parts of the interstate are flooded by the surge. There are multiple casualties."

"What about the other storm?"

Evan went on. "Karl made landfall on the Space Coast half an hour ago. There's no word on damage or casualties there, but you can be sure it will be substantial."

"That means only a hundred and fifty miles separate these two colossal storms. What are you saying on the air?"

"Reporting what we know. Our predictions are crap. None of us have a clue what will happen next."

"Why are you calling me?"

"Because we don't know. None of our models on the Fujiwara Effect fit the circumstances."

"Hold on a second while I pull up the images from the NHC."

Aaron clicked the mouse on his computer. He looked at the

pictures. The storms were almost parallel to each other in the middle of the state. "I see what you mean. Doesn't look like they're gonna spin off independently."

"Right about that, but we have no data on how two major storms will behave over land. I was hoping you might have a guess."

The call was a surprise to Aaron. The crisis of the last day drove anything relating to the academic study of hurricanes from his mind. It wasn't a welcome interruption. The only reason he answered the call was because he thought he might get an immediate forecast for the storms saving him the trouble of checking himself.

"Look, Evan, I don't have time for a conversation. Even less now that I've looked at these images. We're gonna be busy trying to stay alive."

He wasn't the only one thinking this. Angie came around the corner, yelling at him. "What are you doing? You don't have time for this."

Aaron put his hand up and nodded his head. "Angie brought me back to reality, Evan. I gotta go."

"I understand. If you think of something, call me back ... if you can."

Aaron hung up the phone and turned to his wife. "I'm glad we still have power. I got a satellite view of these storms. Both are monsters, and we're right in the middle."

"Tell me something I don't know."

"Knowing the size, speed and exact location of the storms gives me a timeline. Maybe I can figure how many hours, or minutes, we have."

Quietly, Angie closed the doors. "I've been looking over your shoulder for a lot of years. I know more about what's going on than the others."

She pointed at the door. "None of the rest know anything. They probably told themselves they were driving to safety. We both know that's not true. You need to remember when you get everyone together to tell them what you see on those TV images and what it will mean for us."

"I know. You're right, of course."

"Especially since Mason, your strong right arm, will only be able to help a little, or not at all. Then we have Amy. She's beyond terrified and hysterical. She's lost touch with reality."

Aaron took his wife in his arms. "You're not afraid, are you?"

"Oh, I'm afraid. But I also have confidence in you to make the right choices."

"You do lift a fella's spirits."

The two spent a long moment holding each other.

Angie stepped away first. "I guess Mason is still sleeping. When I came in, Ben was talking with Amy. I'm gonna go out and ask who'd like a real breakfast. Those dinky sandwiches didn't fill anybody up. I'll have Sandy help me, then I'll get the whole story from her."

"Good. I need to catch up on as much weather insight as I can. If the power goes out, we'll be blind. I should stay as current as possible. If something is coming in our front door, I'll come tell everyone."

Angie nodded, closing the office doors behind her.

Aaron sat down and turned to his monitors, one for the Weather Channel and another for the National Hurricane Center. He looked at Karl. Evan said it had made landfall within the last hour. He sat up straight and looked again and announced to the monitors. "Maybe I didn't hear him right. Karl is still off shore."

He keyed his remote and rewound to an hour earlier. "Karl did make landfall, but it looks like it abruptly stopped and drifted back to sea."

Aaron put his hands to his eyes and rubbed. In his decades as a meteorologist he had never seen what he was looking at now. "Why?"

He brought up a larger image of Holly. She was still a raging beast but the winds were down and, more significantly, the storm was slowing down. It was moving north at barely five miles an hour. At that rate, it would be through Tampa and north to Homosassa Springs in about twelve hours. Homosassa was forty-five miles due west of The Villages.

He raised his hands in a flash of insight.

My God. I know what's going to happen.

Aaron snatched his phone off the desk and punched Evan Driscoll's number. When he answered, Aaron started talking. "I've looked at the footage from the NHC. Let me tell you what I think is happening and you tell me where I've got it wrong."

"Shoot."

In the next minutes Aaron gave a grim summary of his theory of how the hurricanes were influencing each other and the likely outcome. When he finished, there was silence at the other end.

Evan cleared his throat. "What you said makes more sense than anything I've heard yet. If you're right, this isn't a Florida problem anymore. It's a national emergency."

"Yeah—if I'm right. What are you going to do?"

"We can't go on the air with a forecast from only one person, credible as you are. What we can do is a phone interview and let you tell the whole country what you told me. It'll open the door for others to come forth, pro and con."

"This is one forecast which will be proved right or wrong very quickly. After that, you guys will be overloaded busy."

"No doubt. Give me a minute to see when we can get you in."

Aaron looked at the NHC coverage while he waited. He didn't see anything to change his mind. Ten minutes later he was still waiting.

Finally, Evan came back. "I had to explain, more than once, why I thought we should take a report from you. You've gotten the place full of people with noses stuck to their computer screens, looking at your forecast model. I don't need to. I think you're right."

"Thanks. When are we going on the air?"

"Can you manage a couple hours from now?"

Aaron clinched his teeth in irritation. "We need to get this out right now."

"Look, Doc, you and I have been up all night but most of the rest of the country is still asleep. If you want any kind of an audience, we need to wait until they've had a cup of coffee."

Aaron had to smirk at the use of his nickname from his years at the Weather Channel. "Okay. Two hours it is. I'll have breakfast and call you back."

He ended the call and put his phone on the desk. As he stood up and looked through the window, the haze of night was giving way to gloomy dappled light. Sun-up would go unseen this day. The sky was dark and the clouds dipped close to the ground. Both the wind and the rain had intensified. The palms in his front yard and down the street, flapped in the wind. Rain poured down in gushers. The water running down the street made it looks like the earth was moving. Aaron was glad he lived at the top of a hill. Not a tall hill, maybe fifty feet, but not facing the rising water beginning to fill the low places. Aaron wondered how far the water would rise. He did some quick figuring using his own weather model as a guide. When the answer clicked in his mind, he slammed his hand on the desk in alarm.

This business will get out of hand. It'll get out of hand, and we'll be lucky to live through it.

When he went back to the living room, both Ben and Amy were dozing on the couch. Aaron detoured to the kitchen. Angie and Sandy were making breakfast.

"How you girls doing?"

"We're okay, Dad."

Angie whisked eggs in a bowl. "How much longer are we

gonna have power?"

"I don't know. Don't plan on a long time. You need to cook filling meals whenever you can."

"Breakfast will be ready in a few minutes. Maybe you ought to wake Ben and Amy, and check on Mason."

"I'll do it. Save me some bacon."

Ben gently separated himself from Amy when Aaron came around the corner. "I had a catnap. Have you slept at all, Aaron?"

"Later, if we have time. I'm going to do a telephone interview on the Weather Channel in an hour or so after breakfast."

"What's that all about?"

"I worked there for twenty years. I think I know what these storms are going to do. That's what I'm gonna talk about."

"Are you going to let the rest of us in on your secret?"

"Right after we've eaten breakfast. I planned to include Mason. How much longer will he sleep?"

"Could be awhile."

"I won't wait on him. The rest of you need to know what we can expect to happen today and for the next few days."

Amy stirred and sat up. "What time is it?"

Aaron crossed the room and put out his hand. "Time for breakfast. You can start with a fresh cup of coffee."

"That sounds good. Something normal." She took Aaron's hand as he helped her up.

"As much normal as possible after such an awful day and night." Aaron put his arm around Amy and guided her toward the dining room. "Angie is a great cook. There's nothing like her breakfasts to start the day right."

Amy stepped closer to Aaron and gave him a pale smile. "Thank you for all you've done."

"We're in this together. All of us have a part to play, including you. Do you think you can help us out?"

"I'll try. Tell me what you want me to do."

"Simple. Let's have a nice breakfast, then I'm going to tell you what we all have to do."

Sandy grinned at her father as the two came in. "Dad always makes me feel better when I'm down or having a hard time. He's real smart and thinks of things I haven't."

Angie walked over, a serving dish in both hands. "You have to keep a sharp eye he doesn't steal your bacon."

Amy laughed. "I'm happy to share."

The five settled around the table. Between the eggs and toast disappearing, they had some happy moments talking about things which had nothing to do with the storm. Aaron ate a piece of Amy's bacon. She smiled broadly. "You make me feel like a part of the family."

"We're all part of the family." Aaron pushed his plate aside. "Since that's so, I want to take a few minutes to help you sort out what we can expect to happen next."

Amy wiped the last bit of egg from her plate with a piece of toast. "Aaron's right about you being a great cook. That was a wonderful breakfast."

Angie picked up the dishes from the table, piling them on the counter near the sink. "You're welcome." She turned back to the table. "Now, my alleged smart husband, how about telling us what's going on?"

"Let me grab a pad of paper and an atlas."

Aaron jumped up and hurried to his office. He came back, sat down and drew a map of the state on the pad. He added the two hurricanes on both coasts. Then he held the pad up for the others to see.

"This is about where the storms are right now. Karl is off the Space Coast. Holly has surely reached Tampa and will keep moving north, up the coast. I won't go through the science of having two hurricanes close to one another. I'm not sure any science applies. What we are seeing is unprecedented."

Sandy pointed at the pad. It's gotta get worse, the closer

Holly gets to us."

"I'm afraid so. I wish that was the worst of it. Aaron drew an arrow on the pad, showing Holly continuing north. "These storms are affecting each other. Karl has stopped moving and Holly is slowing considerably. I believe when they get parallel to each other, Holly will also stop as the storms lock themselves in place. Neither will be able to move."

Ben looked up at Aaron. "What's that mean?"

"First, we'll have destructive winds here as Holly comes this way. It will be bad. We're only forty or fifty miles from the west coast. Even so, that won't be the worst. If the storms stall out, as I think they will, we could have torrential rain that lasts for days."

Now Angie chimed in. "How much rain?"

"Measure it in feet instead of inches."

"Are we far enough up this hill to keep from the house flooding?"

"Maybe."

Angie frowned. "What if it doesn't?"

"We might have to leave."

"Where would we go?"

"I don't know."

"My, aren't you a refreshing ray of sunshine."

"No sunshine. I'm sorry. I wish I had better news."

Sandy asked the question Aaron had been thinking about since he first saw the dynamics of the storms. "What happens when the hurricanes start moving again?"

Aaron struggled to explain how he saw the situation. "Think of the storms like a barbell. The bar between them joins the storms together. On each end are hurricanes churning relentlessly. When they do move, they will shift as one. That means the entire eastern part of the country will face a lot of what we will experience here. It could be catastrophic."

Angie nodded in understanding. "Which is why

yousuddenly got interested in talking to the people at the Weather Channel."

"I'm only one guy. I could be wrong. If I'm not, the warning has to be given."

Ben stroked his hair on the back of his head. "I think you're right. What you're saying seems right."

"That's what my colleague at the Weather Channel said. I'm due to do a phone interview in a little while to explain my theory."

Aaron picked up an atlas of the United States and held it up, pointing as he spoke. So, we have two hurricanes, locked into each other. Holly will tear up the panhandle and then move north toward Atlanta. Karl will scour the eastern seaboard including Jacksonville, Savannah, Charleston and the outer banks. In between will be torrential rains of the type we are about to see."

Angie summed it up. "How terrible. What will people do?"

"Get as far away as they can. We can't think much about that now. We have enough to worry about right here."

As if to add an exclamation point to what Aaron said, the room went dark as the power flickered off.

Chapter 10
Insights

Aaron jumped up from the table, grabbing a flashlight as he headed for the garage. He yelled at Angie over his shoulder as he ran out. "Turn off everything. Unplug anything that uses electricity."

He had installed a switch at the fuse box to draw power from the generator. Systematically, he flipped off most of the circuits into the house to make the load more manageable on the generator.

On his way back in, he grabbed a pair of battery-operated lanterns in each hand. He dropped them on the counter, and handed Amy one. "Hold this up for Angie and Sandy as they clear up the dishes." It was good to see her get up and take the lantern. Anything to get her thinking of now and the future rather than to wallow in the past.

"I'll do whatever I can."

Aaron patted her on the cheek. "I know you will."

He snatched his coveralls from a hook in the laundry room, scrambled into it, and flipped the hood over his head. "I'll be right back. I've got to turn on the generator outside."

As he opened the door, the full impact of the storm hit him. It was raining so hard; he could barely see where he was going and the wind battered him. Aaron leaned into it and went around the garage to the side of the house where the generator sat on a concrete pad. It started when he pushed the button. He checked the load on the dials. Even with most of the power off in the house, what remained drove the system at near peak capacity. Aaron made a mental note to go through the house and find anything else to disconnect and make it easier for the equipment to carry the load. He sorted through the things which would be a priority—refrigerator, microwave, a couple outlets in the kitchen to plug in cell phones, and damned little else.

Angie waited at the front door with a dry towel. "I pulled the plug on everything I could. It's dark in here. We need more lanterns."

"I'll get some. We also need to light candles to save on batteries. Are you done in the kitchen?"

"Sandy and Amy are finishing up. You're pretending she's helping is working. I think she's trying as hard as she can to please you."

"Good. Let's build on that. Try to transfer some of her new-found loyalty to yourself. Then I can work on the bigger problems. Where's Ben?"

"He took one of the lanterns and went in to check on Mason."

Aaron looked at his watch. "I have a little time before I try to talk to Evan in Atlanta. I'll go look at Mason myself."

Ben was taking Mason's blood pressure when Aaron came in. He turned and smiled. "His pressure is better now." He tapped the IV bag. "He lost quite a bit of blood from the injury. All I have is this saline solution."

Mason was sprawled face down on the bed. "How long before he wakes up?"

"I hope he sleeps for as long as he can. How much time do we have before conditions deteriorate so much, I have to get him up?"

"When I last looked at the storms, Holly had slowed to about five miles an hour. I estimate it will be twelve hours before it comes far enough north for its winds to cause us major problems. I can't look at the storms now with the power out, so a lot might have changed. It could be completely different. My super-duper idea on what will happen, might turn out to be total bullshit."

"You don't believe that, do you?"

"I may be wrong, but I'm not uncertain."

"Not that I know anything, but I don't think you're wrong.

Keep doing what you believe is right. One more thing, Aaron. Thanks a lot for the help with Amy. At least she's busy and not stewing about our drive up here."

"We should keep her busy, let her know she's part of the team. Include her in any major decisions.

Aaron paused, wondering how much he should say. To him, the nurse had the calm confidence of a surgeon. He decided to promote him. "In any case, Doc, we'll know more when I talk to Atlanta. The countdown begins then, all around thinking how to survive. You do understand how serious the situation is?"

"Not as much as you. I'll take your word for it. Only tell me enough to make an informed judgement."

"I might tell you more than you want to hear."

Ben gave a gloomy shrug and turned back to Mason. "Whatever."

Aaron checked his watch again. "I'm gonna make the call now." He slipped out of the room, closing the door silently.

There was an empty feeling to his office when he returned. His TV monitors were dark and the room was quiet. Aaron sat a lantern on his desk and picked up his phone. It took ten minutes of dialing and redialing before he got through.

Mercifully, Evan finally answered. "I'm glad we waited the two hours. The progress of the storms is proving you right. After we charted your model, we sent it on to the NHC. Now they are using it in their broadcasts. I don't think you were the only one with the same idea, but you were the fella who stuck his neck out first."

"The power went out here. I have no data stream. Bring me up to date."

"Holly is moving slowly at five miles an hour. She's nine or ten hours south and west of you, still over water. Karl is still stationary off the Space Coast. It's the screwiest thing I've ever seen."

"Me too, but the circumstances fit my forecast."

"Stand by. We'll be going on the air in a few minutes."

Aaron concentrated while he waited, collecting his thoughts.

Soon enough Evan was back on the line and began the broadcast. "In the past couple days, we've talked a lot about the Fujiwara Effect. That is, the behavior of hurricanes that come together. The foremost expert on the Fujiwara Effect is our own Doctor Aaron Colson, the former chief meteorologist at the Weather Channel, now retired and living in The Villages in Florida. He's in the middle of this. Power is out at his home, but we were able to contact him by phone. Good morning, Aaron."

"I wish it was a good morning, Evan."

"Can you explain your forecast we talked about earlier?"

"I'll try. Typically, when two hurricanes get close, they exhibit what's called the Fujiwara Effect. They dance around each other and then either spin away in different directions, or the bigger storm absorbs the smaller. I believe the Fujiwara Effect is still active here. However, the two hurricanes can't dance together because the Florida land mass is in between them."

"How does that affect the behavior of the storms?"

"These are two huge hurricanes. The circulation of wind and rain in the bands extending outward are influencing both storms. In a few hours they will be parallel to each other across the central Florida. Karl has stopped moving off the Space Coast and Holly will drift north and also stop. The hurricanes will be locked in a kind of Mexican standoff."

"According to your model the hurricanes could stall out for days."

"Something like this has happened before. In 1998 Hurricane Mitch hit Central America and stalled over Nicaragua for a week. It killed 20,000 people and destroyed 300,000 homes. And that was one hurricane. We have two."

"Eventually the hurricanes will move. What will happen then?"

"Their winds will keep them locked. They will move north. Holly will make landfall in the Florida panhandle and then move toward you, Evan. The people of Atlanta need to know what's coming."

"What about Karl?"

"It will likely move along the east coast with destructive winds, and a major storm surge for coastal cities like Jacksonville, Savannah and Charleston. The damage could be catastrophic."

"What about the states between the hurricanes?"

"Torrential rain for a long time. There will be flooding everywhere."

"When you first suggested such outcomes to me a couple of hours ago, your forecast and storm models seemed inconceivable. Now, the rest of us have come to believe you got it right."

"Mores the pity. I wish I was looking at something else. We have the Fujiwara Effect in spades. We'll have the fury of both storms in central Florida in a few hours. I'll be measuring rainfall here in feet. Much of the east coast can expect the same in a few days."

Aaron knew Evan had already digested his forecast. There was still a pause on his end.

"Thanks very much for your insight. You've given us an understanding of this unprecedented weather phenomenon."

With the interview finished, Aaron had a private moment with Evan. "Now we've got a handle on these guys, I want to know your estimate of what we can expect here when Holly moves further north."

"I'm only guessing but it looks like Category 3 strength in The Villages."

"That's still 120 mile-per-hour winds. How much time do I have?"

"Eight or nine hours at her current speed and strength."

"Terrific. Thanks, Evan. I've got to go."

❖

Evan Driscoll hung up the phone and spun his seat around to face the crowd in the studio who had gathered while he did the interview.

He spoke to his colleague Jim Meyers. "I doubt we will be able to speak to him again."

Jim nodded his head. "Let's hope it isn't forever."

"Aaron knows exactly what's ahead. No reason to warn him, but I think we should sound the alarm for the east coast."

"We need to watch and see if Holly comes to a stop a few hours from now. If it does, I'll bet everyone will get on board.

Evan looked at the images of the two hurricanes again. "Boy. Are these monsters going to make a mess. Aaron and his family are in big trouble."

Aaron put down the phone. He sat back in his chair and realized how mortally tired he was. The rest must be in the same shape. They all needed some sleep. Right after he brought them up to date. He got up and came out of his office, lantern in hand. Angie was there to meet him.

"Anything new?"

"Only that my forecast is being more accepted by the minute. Can we get everyone together? I need to tell them the latest."

"What about Mason?"

"Is he still sleeping?"

"I think so."

"Let him sleep. Everybody will join him in a few minutes."

"I'll gather them up."

The five sat back at the dining room table. The glow of the lanterns shed an eerie light through the room.

"The good news is my forecast for these storms is correct. The bad news is my forecast for these storms is correct. Holly is running up the gulf coast. It will be here in about eight hours.

"I've done all the preparations I could think of, so we can

only wait. We haven't slept very well in days and not at all in the past twenty-four hours. We should take this chance and get some sleep."

Amy shook a gloomy head. "I don't know if I can sleep."

"You have to. We all need rest. There's no telling when the opportunity will come again."

The others around the table were silent. Aaron put his hands on the table. "Okay. Ben and Amy can have the spare bedroom. Sandy can sleep with Angie in our bed. I'll settle down on the couch in my office. Have a good rest."

Aaron watched them get up and slip quietly away. When he was alone, he took a lantern and retreated to his office. He kicked off his shoes, pulled off his wrinkled shorts and lay down on the couch, grabbing a blanket.

He closed his eyes and was asleep before he knew it.

Chapter 11
Holly's Howling Winds

<u>Mid-day Tuesday</u>
The roar of the wind dipped deep into Mason's consciousness. He stirred and tried to get up. Pain rocketed through him. Slowly he pushed himself off the bed and onto his knees on the floor. He forced himself to his feet, then sat down gently on the edge of the bed, shaking his head violently to clear his mind. He leaned away from the mass of bandages on his butt.

Shot in the ass. I'll never live it down.

He had no idea how long he'd slept or what had happened while he did. He stood up again and flipped the light switch. Nothing. *Powers out.*

Mason switched on the battery-operated lantern on the end table. He traced the IV tube down from the empty bag. With a nonchalant motion he pulled the needle out and rubbed his arm. Then he went over and opened the door. It hurt to walk. It hurt to sit. Hell, it hurt without any help from him. The door to the other bedroom was closed. Mason went down the hall and into the living room.

Where is everyone? What's going on?

A new gust of wind made the house tremble. He went to the window and looked out. Palm fronds, tree branches, and other debris bounced along the street and yards crashing into houses before blowing away. It was a terrifying sight.

He turned to the closed office door and pushed it open. Aaron snored under a blanket on the couch.

"Wake up, Aaron."

Now it was Aaron's turn to climb up out of a deep sleep. He rolled over and rubbed his eyes. "Mason? Is that you?"

"In the flesh, so to speak. What's going on?"

Aaron sat up and rubbed his eyes again. "What time is it?"

Mason glanced at the wall clock. "A little after twelve.

Guess that's in the afternoon."

Aaron got up and grabbed Mason by the shoulders. "How are you feeling?"

"Groggy and my butt hurts. Other than that, I think I'm all right."

"That's a relief. I was wondering if I'd have to ride out this hurricane on my own."

"What about the others? Where's Sandy?"

"Probably still asleep in my room with her mother. I sent everyone to bed hours ago. That screaming wind means it's time to roust them."

"Are you going to tell me what's going on?"

Aaron spent a few minutes catching Mason up on everything which had happened while he slept. His eyes grew larger with each sentence Aaron spoke.

"Sounds like I missed a bunch. What do you want me to do now?"

"Go in and wake Sandy. I expect Mom will get up too. I'm going to see if I can find a local radio station and try to catch up. Mason went off.

Aaron switched on his radio and tuned for signals. Presently the static stopped and a voice crackled to life.

...for all people in central Florida. Hurricane winds exceeding one hundred and ten miles per hour will continue for the next hour. If you are in the open or in a car, you must find safe shelter immediately. If you are in safe shelter, stay there. Do not go outside. Stay tuned for further updates.

This is a hurricane warning for all people in central Florida. Hurricane winds exceeding one hun...

Aaron recognized the repeat of a recorded message. He turned the radio down. When he came out of his office into the living room, he plowed into Ben coming from the hall.

"Oomph. Oops. S'cuse me, Doc. I was listening to the radio."

"What did it say?"

Aaron pointed to the window. "Those winds out there will keep up and get worse for an hour."

"What do I do?"

"We need to get everyone up, dressed and gathered in the safest room in the house."

"I'll see about Amy." He stopped as Mason came out of the master bedroom with Sandy. The medic in him turned to his patient. "You need to be careful and not jar that wound. You don't want to rip out those staples and start bleeding again."

"I'll do the best I can."

Angie bustled out of the bedroom wearing a one-piece coverall with a zipper in the front. "Ready."

"I'll get Amy." Ben hurried off.

Aaron pointed at his wife's outfit. "I better put on my coveralls."

"This is a good time to change."

Aaron looked at himself and gasped. He went past the laundry room, snatched his coveralls and rushed to the bedroom.

Angie couldn't resist. "Blue polka-dot shorts should never be seen in public."

Sandy laughed and hugged Mason, who turned aside to keep her from bumping his leg and butt. "Oh. I'm sorry, honey. I forgot your bad spot."

Aaron couldn't hear anymore conversation. He rummaged through a dresser drawer and pulled out a pair of shorts. He slipped them on and then snatched the coveralls from the bed. He stepped into it and zipped up the front. Then he went to the bathroom, picked up a cloth and wiped his face. "It's getting hot in here." After picking up a stack of the waterproof slickers, he returned to the living room to join the others.

He came in smiling his best. "There're coveralls for all of

you. They're waterproof and have a hood." He demonstrated by pulling the hood over his head.

Aaron looked around. "Where's Ben and Amy?"

As he spoke, Ben led Amy into the room. The little smile on her face vanished when she saw Mason. She melted into her husband, who angled her to a nearby couch.

Ben turned back to Mason. "Sorry. She can't seem to let go of the scene at the gas station."

"She acts like she's suffering from PTSD."

"Exactly."

Mason frowned and looked down at the floor. "I know about that stuff."

Aaron walked over to Amy and handed her a coverall. "This is for you. I wish we had time to talk, but we must get to safety right now. I need you to concentrate on what's going on around us. Can you do that for me?"

Amy looked up, wiped away a tear, and took the coveralls. "I'll try."

Aaron turned to the others. "Let's get to the laundry room."

The laundry room was between the kitchen and the garage. There were folding chairs against the wall. Aaron talked while he helped unfold them. "This is the safest room in the house. It has rooms around it. Also, it's on the corner of the house away from the worst storm winds."

The others pulled their coveralls over their clothes and sat down. In such a small room, the six were touching each other's knees.

The fury of the wind outside rose to a higher register.

Sandy turned her head to the sound and shouted. "The wind was incredible on the drive up here. This is worse."

Aaron took Amy's hand. She scooted closer and put her arms around his waist. "I'm so scared; like before."

He put an arm around her. "Yeah, me too."

She looked up at Aaron. "I thought I was the only one."

"This would scare the shit out of anybody. Where did you get the idea you're alone?"

"I don't know. I thought I was."

"Well, you're not. Start paying attention, dammit. Look at my daughter. Does she look calm and composed?"

Amy peered across at Sandy. She had the same wild look on her face. "I guess not. It shouldn't make me feel better, but it does."

"Don't feel bad about being petrified shitless. Welcome to the club."

Something else rumbled over the roar of the wind. It was wrenching, tearing sounds, echoing nature's destruction.

Sandy looked around her. "What's that noise, Dad?"

"The wind is blowing trees down and roofs off houses, I'll bet. Everybody hang on, I'm gonna take a look."

Aaron went back to his office and stared out the big window facing the street. Rubble filled the air. Through the curtains of rain, he saw the roofs were gone from the three closest houses across the street. One of them had only a few walls still standing. These houses were facing more into the wind. The destruction made Aaron grimace. His home was only marginally less exposed and only because his walls were concrete.

In the distance, Aaron saw the outline of two people struggling up the street. He could only imagine what they'd gone through. He started planning on adding them to his group, when the roof of a house behind him tore away. It spun in the air and then plunged down. It fell directly on the couple swallowing them as if they had never existed.

He gulped down a lump in his throat. "God. God." The first time he shouted. The second time he prayed.

When he got back to the laundry room, five faces turned toward him.

What to say.

He plopped down. Amy grabbed his hand and squeezed.

Angie wrapped her arm around his.

He used the hand Amy wasn't clutching and pointed toward the roof. "It ain't good. We can only hope to ride this out." He pointed at the wall clock. "The recorded radio message said these winds would last an hour. It's been a half hour since I heard it. Our odds get better with every passing minute."

Aaron didn't say more. He let his suggestion of time passing capture the attention of the others on the clock. They stared at it hypnotically. The screaming wind made conversation impossible.

The next thirty minutes moved like a glacier. Mason spoke first. "Is it my wishful thinking or is the wind dying down?"

"I wanted someone else to mention it first since I wasn't sure and it's more hearing and feeling than knowing."

"Meaning the house isn't shaking so much."

"That, and noise of the wind is less."

"How much longer should we wait?"

"Let's listen for a while."

Ten minutes later, Aaron got up. "The wind is definitely falling off. Let me take a peek outside."

Leaving the room was more to give Aaron time to think than to see, again, the catastrophe at his front door. He still looked. There was even less visibility. A very frightening torrential rain filled the air with pieces of houses. He shook his head. A large part of his alert forecast must be right. His prediction said Holly's hurricane force winds would abate as the eye passed to the north, replaced by this furious rain. That appeared to be happening. What he didn't know was how long the two storms would dump rain in middle of the state.

Hope for the best. Plan for the worst.

He went back to the laundry room. "Hear how the sound of rain on the roof is louder than the wind? It's blowing less and raining more. I don't know what's worse. At least we still have a roof over our heads. I..."

Abruptly the roar of the wind rose above the rain.

Aaron jerked his head to follow the agonized cracking of wood breaking. "The rafters are giving way. Cover your heads and hang on."

In a single brutal gust, the roof ripped away. The bedrooms, office and half the living room gaped wide-open to the elements. The six people in the laundry room rocked back in the face of a hundred-mile-an hour blast of wind and rain. Everything not tied down erupted in a hail of airborne debris, bouncing off the walls, floors and people. Screams of fear echoed through the little room. Aaron put his arms around Angie and Amy to shield them from the worst of it. A flying soup can slammed him on the side of the head. He grunted in pain and held on. He could hear the others hollering as flying, falling objects hit them.

It seemed endless but after a few minutes the wind died away, leaving the rain falling in a torrent. Aaron got up and looked around to see what was left. The roof still covered the kitchen, garage, half the living room and the laundry. The spray from the rain washed across his face. The huge hole over the living room was letting in a lot of water, soaking everything.

It's nearly as bad as being outside.

He could see the black skies through the living room. Beyond that, only bare walls still stood. The wind had scoured out all the furnishings, like a cook washing out a sink.

The shock of raw nature slamming them was passing. What remained were the bruises, welts, cuts and lacerations.

Blood dripped to the floor.

Chapter 12
Digging In

Evan Driscoll stared at his computer screen. He'd been that way for half an hour.

Jim Meyers walked over to his station. "You're due back on the air in a few minutes."

"I know."

"What are you going to say?"

"Both these storms are behaving exactly as Aaron said. I hope he and has family are all right."

"They had Cat 3 winds in central Florida when Holly's eye pulled up parallel with Karl and stopped moving."

"The rain between the storms has got to be a drenching downpour."

"No doubt. They'll keep pounding Florida until the storms start moving again. Any guess on how long that will be?"

"Not a clue. Aaron said it could be a couple days."

"The alert you issued for the eastern seaboard has millions of people trying to get as far away as they can."

"I hope they have the time. I hope the man responsible for giving them the time, is still alive."

Aaron wiped the blood from his eyes and looked around. "Is everyone okay?"

The others sat up, feeling themselves for the places that hurt. There were cuts, bumps, bruises and torn coveralls among them all. Amy moaned a little as she rubbed her fingers across the deep cut on her cheek.

Aaron put his arm around her and swung his eyes toward Ben. "Amy needs some help."

"You first, Aaron. That gouge on your head is still bleeding."

Aaron put his hand to the side of his forehead. His fingers

came away, dripping blood. "It didn't hurt so bad until now." He grabbed a towel from the washing machine and pressed it to his head.

Ben started to get up, then sat back down. "I left my bag in the bedroom."

Mason looked into the living room, rain drenching the floor through the rip in the ceiling. "I think that whole part of the house is gone."

"I had a box of medical supplies in the SUV. I hope it didn't get blown away."

Aaron dabbed away at his head. "I pulled our car out of the garage and drove it between houses on the side with the generator. I drove your car in behind. I wanted to shield the generator from the wind and give a little cover for the vehicles."

"Our bags are still in the SUV, Dad."

Mason patted Sandy on her leg. "Ben and I'll go get them."

"The wind is still blowing at near gale force. You can probably manage that. The biggest problem will be the rain." Aaron stood up. "Can I help you?"

Mason made a humorless smile. "Yeah. How do we get out of the house?"

It wasn't a dumb question. Aaron thought for a few seconds. He stepped out of the laundry room and hugged a nearby living room wall, shoving away a couch, to dodge most of the rain. When he came around a corner, he saw the walls of the hallway to the front door were still standing. He went back to join Mason and Ben, sorting the conditions they faced in his head.

"You can still get out the front door. Go that way. I don't want to lift the garage door. It's still dry in there. We need to rethink our housing. We'll turn the garage into a living room and convert the living room into a place to sleep."

Mason looked over at the drenched room. "How you gonna do that?"

"I've got a big tent in the garage. Angie thought I was nuts for buying it. We'll pitch it in the living room and nail it down. It'll divert the rain off the side open to the sky and keep the other side dry. The walls still standing on both sides of the living room will keep the tent from blowing away"

Mason frowned in hesitation. "That might work if we can find enough anchor points for the tent."

Aaron waved away the objection. "I got lots of big spikes. I'll go pull the tent into the living room while you guys get the bags."

Ben nodded, he and Mason pulled the hoods over their coveralls and headed for the front door.

Angie followed her husband into the garage. "After I help you lug this tent into the house, what do you want me to do?"

"Check the kitchen. See if we still have power to the refrigerator."

"Alright, but the storm blew away every place in the house with clothes, the stuff in the bathrooms and most of the linens. All we have left are the clean clothes I stacked on the washer."

"Check around and see what's left right after we get the tent."

It took both Aaron and Angie to haul the heavy tent into a corner of the gaping living room. Aaron was glad they had the waterproof coveralls. The rain blew relentlessly on them. The cloth he was using to dab his head was soaked through. Bloody streaks appeared each time he blotted the cloth. The wound continued to bleed.

Mason and Ben burst through the front door. Ben carried a large cooler; Mason came behind lugging a couple suitcases. "I told you. I'm fine. Just a pain in the ass."

Aaron let Ben walk into the kitchen and then asked on his own. "How about it?"

"I didn't pull a staple. It still hurts." He pulled the bags to a stop. "I'll get the rest of it."

Mason left and Aaron went back to the kitchen where Ben

was taking an inventory. "How much of the stuff in your bag can you replace from what you have here?"

"Almost all of it." He picked up a stethoscope and a blood pressure sleeve. "In the doctor world, these are like pens. You can never have too many."

Aaron smiled. *No worries in his department.*

Mason plodded through the soaking rain, back to the SUV. He'd left the rear hatch open to make it easier to grab the last bags. He hadn't been entirely truthful to Aaron about the wound in his butt. He might have pulled a staple. It sure hurt like it. He pulled the bags from the car, closed the hatch and started back to the front door.

As he pulled the suitcases, he looked around at the staggering destruction. The roofs of almost all the houses he could see were gone. Some of the homes blown down to their foundations. He wondered who else had survived. Certainly, no other people were wandering around. He went through the front door.

Aaron was waiting for him. "This tent we hauled in, opens up to twelve by sixteen feet. It's an army tent. Ever seen it before?"

"It was a common tent we used a lot. I've seen them set up. Only done it myself a few times."

"Think you can figure it out and supervise the rest of us pitching this one?"

"I guess. This rain will make it a big job."

"The sooner we get it done, the sooner we'll be able to dry it out inside."

"This is nuts. How's it going to help?"

Mason knew his father-in-law was thinking of what to say as he stared straight into his eyes. He appreciated that, as Aaron answered. "So far, all my predictions on these storms' behavior have happened here." He pointed out the window. "We had the hurricane winds which must have done catastrophic damage throughout The Villages, judging by what we can see right out there."

"Maybe we're through the worst of it."

"Then I would breathe a huge sigh of relief. But what if it isn't? What if the whole terrible forecast continues to play out?"

"We get a lot of rain?"

"Not a lot, Mason, a deluge of biblical proportions which could go on for days."

"You think that's why we need the tent?"

"Right. You can't expect three couples to live, work and sleep, in only the garage for an unknown number of days."

The logic clicked in Mason's head. "This tent will be the bedroom, our most private place."

Aaron swept his hands in conclusion. "You read the instructions while I round up some cheap labor."

Painful memories scorched Amy's mind. Every minute since the first storm clouds appeared one horror after another had piled up.

At the core of her consciousness lay a deep, dark pool of guilt. None of the panic of the drive and the unspeakable scene at the gas station would have happened if she had gotten some gas. The guilt clouded her mind and made it hard to do anything.

It helped that the others didn't act like they blamed her. Especially Aaron. His calm voice and gentle hand gave her some relief.

"Amy—Amy—Amy."

She realized a voice was speaking to her. It was Aaron, sitting down beside her.

"Amy, are you with us?"

"My cheek hurts."

"Sorry. But my cut is bigger than yours." He smiled and pulled away the towel to show her his gash.

"That's terrible. Did Ben look at it?"

"Not yet. Right now, we're trying to put up a tent to get us out of the wet. Can you help?"

"Sure. Take my hand."

Aaron paused, then looked her in the eye. "You don't look like you've had much sleep."

Amy told the truth. "Not much. I can't get that man being shot out of my head."

"It's the kind of thing nobody should have to see. Getting over it is tough. Mason is the expert on that. You should ask him."

"He's the reason I have the memory. Maybe he didn't have a choice, but he still killed that guy."

"Nobody knows that better than Mason. He served in the Middle East. Several tours, I think. What happened last night was not the first time for him. His training saved your life. You do know that, don't you?"

"I guess."

"Alright. Try this. We've survived a major hurricane. What comes next is rain and more rain. Unless we plug the leak from the roof ripping away, we'll be wet and miserable. The tent is to make part of the house livable again. Are you going to help or not?"

Amy looked at Aaron's serious eyes. She realized she had to help no matter how she felt. Also, she didn't want to disappoint Aaron. "Show me what to do."

"That's the spirit. Come on along. We'll get started."

Putting up a tent inside a house, with half the roof torn away, took two hours of grueling labor by all six. It was a relief to be out of the rain under the big space, but water still poured down the sides and onto the floor. Aaron got an ax from the garage and knocked holes in the floor to give a place for the water to run. In another hour, the new sleeping area was dry. Angie and Sandy collected every dry rug left and spread them over the floor.

Aaron stepped back, surveying the improvised room. "The

walls still standing works like a box wrapped around the tent. The wind is still strong but I don't think it'll blow everything away. Having a dry place to relax and sleep will be more comfortable for us."

The rain made a heavy drumming on the tent roof. Angie looked up at it. "How long are we going to have this heavy rain?"

"Frankly, I don't know."

"You didn't have any trouble telling everyone on the Weather Channel what you thought would happen and it has. If that was right, what would come next?"

"Torrential rains will flood central Florida until the storms begin drifting north."

Mason eased onto the seat of a folding chair from the laundry room. He waved his arms around. "This will work for us. What about the people who lost their homes?"

Aaron shook his head. "If they survived the storm, they'll be exposed to this downpour."

"We oughta go out and see what's left."

"Not you, bub. You took a beating setting up this tent. Why don't you rest while I go out and take a look?"

"I'm okay, Aaron."

Amy waved her hands. "Why would anyone go outside? We're safe in here."

Mason smiled at her. "We can't stay holed up in our safe place. We have to know what's going on outside that might help or hurt us."

Ben picked up his medical bag. "There could be injured people out there. I'll go look."

Sandy got up from the floor. "I'll go with you."

Aaron zipped up his coveralls. Angie rushed over, grabbing his arm. "You've taken a beating yourself. How about the old boy getting a little rest himself?"

"You guys be careful out there."

Angie pointed toward the garage. "Why don't you show

Mason and Amy the supplies and stuff you've stored?"

"Yeah, Aaron. I thought the tent you pulled out of nowhere was pretty handy. What else have you squirreled away?"

"Come on along. I'll show you."

Amy looked back and forth between Mason and Aaron. She wrapped her hand around Aaron's arm. Angie handed her a pen and a pad of paper. "Take this. Aaron likes to make lists."

Mason led the way, holding a lantern above his head.

Aaron followed Amy. It was still dark and gloomy in the garage. He slapped his hand to his head. "It's too dark to see. Hold on a minute, I'll go get another lantern."

The kitchen door closed behind him.

Amy retreated to a far corner. She couldn't look at Mason.

He looked at her and took a deep breath. "I killed that guy."

"I know. I saw the whole thing. It was horrible."

"How hard do you think it was for the guy who had to pull the trigger?"

Amy looked sharply at Mason. "You were so calm and unemotional."

"Only because my training and experience as a soldier helped me push past the moment. This wasn't the first time."

Amy didn't feel any better.

"Our country has a military so nice people like you, never have to witness such things. I wish I didn't have so many. For me, I still faced an enemy and the bullets were still flying, so I had to keep going. The storms are the enemy now, and we have to keep going no matter what pictures are in our head."

Amy stared blankly. "It was so terrible I'll never forget it."

"No, you won't. When you're an old woman, your grandchildren will ask you why you never talk about the hurricanes. You'll say, 'Because the memories are so awful.' Then they'll say, 'But grandma, it happened so many years in the past.' Then you'll say, 'It wasn't years, it was only a moment ago.'"

Amy fell back onto a wooden box. Tears dripped down her cheeks. "I can't live with this."

"Yes, you can. Thousands of us faced the same kind of gruesome circumstances. Most of us found ways to blot it out. Especially if there was more of the same coming at us. I guarantee there's more shitty stuff coming our way. You need to concentrate on the next thing to do, things that will help our situation. File your grim memories into a classified archive in your mind, with a big, 'Do not Disturb' sign on it. Then go to work and don't think about it."

"Do you think it'll do any good."

"No promises, but it works for me. These days I cook and run a restaurant. I also put up a tent, like you helped do. How many times did the gruesome images come to mind while you were doing it?"

Amy stared away for a moment, then turned back to Mason. "Not at all."

"See? The incident at the gas station happened less than a day ago, and you were able to turn off the memory. Your rational mind tells you I had no choice. It's the raw emotions flooding your head. From now on, let everyone see how impressively relaxed and unruffled you are. That way they can start worrying about things besides you."

Amy wiped away her tears and sat up straighter. "You're right. Funny. Now we've talked about it, I don't feel so bad."

"Of course not. It's the people who don't talk about who have the hardest time."

The rain covered Sandy like a blanket as she and Ben stepped out the front door. This was her first look at the carnage which used to be a quiet residential neighborhood. The shattered remains of a house roof blocked the street. Nearly every home she could see was severely damaged, their roofs blown away. The frame-built homes were worse. Their wooden walls collapsed in the wind with the roofs gone. Only those homes built of cement block and stucco, like Aaron's, had withstood the worst of the storm.

Sandy yelled over the roar of the rain. "Dad said it was bad. He was being easy on us. Most of these houses are ripped to pieces. Where should we go?"

"We'll check the nearest ones first."

"What if we find somebody?"

"Depends on whether they're alive or not."

"How awful." Sandy followed Ben down the driveway and into the debris-strewn street.

They had only gone a few steps when both stopped in their tracks. Lying the middle of the street were the bodies of two people. There was no blood. The pair—a man and a woman—were pale and white as if Mother Nature wanted no evidence of life left behind. Sandy put her hand to her mouth in shock.

Ben walked to the bodies and checked them. He looked up with a sad shake of his head. "They're dead."

"How did they get here?"

Ben peered into the gloom of the storm. "From all this rubble, I'd say a roof fell on them as they were running for safety. Then the wind blew the roof again and it flipped over to where it is now, leaving these two, lying exposed."

"I guess this means we're going to find more."

"Very likely. But there could be people alive in this mess. Let's keep checking."

Sandy followed Ben for the next half-hour as he gingerly poked through the ruins of more houses. They found seven more lifeless bodies.

With each grim discovery, Sandy grew more nauseated. The last couple lay smashed against a fragment of a wall. They died in each other's arms. The sight was more than Sandy could stand. She leaned over and violently vomited. Finally, she stood up, wiping her mouth. The vomit washed away in the rain, leaving her with the sour taste.

"You okay?"

"I'm sorry. I couldn't help myself. I've never seen such terrible things. What are we going to do?"

"Nothing right now. It's getting dark. When we get back inside, we need to talk about setting up a temporary morgue. Unprocessed bodies, laying in the open like this, are septic and a health hazard."

"Are we going to find bodies in every house?"

"It doesn't look good. Let's get out of the rain."

Ben led the way as they picked their way through the shattered wood, glass, furniture, clothing and piles of household goods that lay everywhere. It was a relief for Sandy to get back inside.

When she came through the door, she realized how incredibly fortunate they had been. What looked like a grubby tent when she went out, now seemed like the snuggest place in the world.

Aaron and Angie were at the front door to greet them. Angie passed out dry towels. Sandy sagged into her mother's arms.

Ben pulled off his coveralls and turned to Aaron. "We found nine bodies out there. I left them where they lay, but we can't leave them like that."

"How many houses did you check?"

"A half dozen or so, the remains of them. Not much left standing, except this place. I've never seen it rain so hard."

Sandy looked at her father with stark terror in her eyes. "There were dead people everywhere we looked. Are we the only ones left alive?"

"I don't know, honey. Be glad we are."

Heavy pounding shook the front door.

Chapter 13
Refugees

Aaron jerked his head is surprise. "Did you see anybody walking around out there?"

Ben shrugged his shoulders. "No, we didn't."

"Somebody must have seen you." Aaron went to the door and opened it.

Before he could say a word, two dripping and obviously terrified seniors rushed in. Aaron recognized them as Mike and Molly Barker from farther down the street. He closed the door.

Mike Barker stomped his feet and brushed water from his face. "We saw the flashlights and two people going through the ruined homes. I can tell you it was a welcome sight. Up until now we didn't think anybody had survived."

"We almost didn't. What about your place?"

"The wind took our roof, not that it made much difference. There're a couple feet of water in our house. We're flooded out."

"The rain is flowing down the hill toward your place. It's good you got out when you did. I think it's going to rain for quite a while. No telling how high the water will get. Anyway, you're safe now. Angie, do we have any dry clothes?"

"I think I can round up something for you to wear." She put her arm around Molly's shoulders. "I'm so sorry about your house. Come in. Let's get you dry." She picked up a couple of handy towels and gave them to the two neighbors.

Shortly, Angie found some dry clothes. She handed them to Molly and waved her arm around at the tent. "Close quarters, but it's dry. We'll go to the garage so you can change in private."

"Thanks so much."

Aaron motioned to the others.

When they were alone in the garage, he gave a grim assessment. "While Ben and Sandy were outside, I tried my cell phone. There's no signal at all, and even if I could get through, I don't think anyone would, or could, come to help."

Mason nodded his head in understanding. "That leaves only the emergency radio channels. Have you been able to speak to anyone?"

"Not yet." He held up his two-way radio. "There's a lot of chatter on channels up and down the emergency frequencies. Mostly it's police, fire and other rescue workers trying to move survivors to places of safety. I tried to raise anybody on this radio and got nothing."

"Find anything that sounds like a command and control frequency?"

"I did. It sounds like the emergency broadcast system. The signal is steady and free of a lot of cross talk. You can hear what I heard."

Aaron clicked on the radio and turned up the volume. A tired sounding man was speaking.

At the present time, all power is out over central Florida. Cell towers have either been knocked down by the hurricane winds or flooded out. There are no estimates when these services will be restored.

The heavy rain has flooded streets and tunnels throughout The Villages and inundated an unknown but large number of homes at lower ground levels.

All first responders are busy with rescue operations or working to establish safe shelters. Residents should seek safety on hills at higher elevations above water levels and help each other until emergency crews can reach you. There is a need for anyone with boats to move people to recreation centers still above water. No two-way traffic is permitted on this frequency. Tune to 29.7 to seek and offer aid.

Aaron turned the radio down as the announcer read a list of emergency shelters. "We're on top of one of the hills. I tried to get through on the other frequency but couldn't speak to anyone because of the cross talk. With the roads flooded, the only way we could get any help is by helicopter, or a boat. We're stuck until something shows up."

Sandy clicked her tongue in mock disapproval. "I can't believe you don't have a collapsible boat packed away in all these supplies."

"The need looks so obvious now. I should have thought of it. The best I can do is a few blow-up mattresses."

Mason waved his hand as if to get everyone back to the issues at hand. "Okay, what do we do now?"

Aaron looked around at the others. "The Barkers' are the first. We'll find others with little or nothing and no place else to go. The six of us are gonna get spread thin taking care of these people."

Angie shoved her shoulder into her husband's arm. "How thin?"

"Finding survivors is good and bad. On the one hand they can pitch in on the cooking, keeping our emergency shelter dry and secure and helping others. On the other hand, more people eating, sleeping and living with us is tougher. Our supplies are limited. We'll have to ration everything."

Ben added his own conclusions. "We may find others who need medical attention. My ability to treat them is limited. I have basic supplies of medicine, bandages and so forth, but if any of them have serious injuries, the only place to provide even minimal care is in this garage."

Sandy looked around. "How many people are we talking about?"

Aaron walked to the middle of the garage and spread his arms open. "Let's start with the two we have. There's no more room in the tent with the six of us already packed in there."

He pointed around. "A lot of the stuff in here is for something besides an emergency. We need to clean it out, stack it outside."

Mason took in the scene. "To do that you're going to have to open a garage door. How much water will get in here?"

"The garage faces north out of the wind. Maybe the eaves will keep most of the rain out. In any case we don't have much choice."

"What do you intend to do with the golf cart?"

"Pull it out on the driveway. I hope it stays dry enough to start if we find a reason to use it."

"Let's get started."

"It's getting dark. We can wait until morning. Besides, we need to eat something. I'm sure the Barkers' are hungry too. They must be exhausted from the strain of the past couple of days."

"Thanks a lot, Dad. I wasn't hungry till you said it. Now I could eat a horse."

Aaron gave Sandy a hug and then went on. "From now on, we need to mount a watch. Everything we have is jury rigged and will need attention. Plus, more people could find us. One of us needs to be awake, alert and watching all the time."

Mason sat down, gingerly, on a sack of lawn fertilizer. "That won't be so hard. Six of us. Only four-hour watches."

"I'll leave the schedule to you. Don't put yourself at the top of the list. You're still walking wounded and need to lay back down and rest."

"I won't argue with that. Since you embarrassed everyone with your polka-dot shorts, you get the first shift."

Aaron laughed. "I'll get right to work, after I have something to eat."

"Is there enough power to run the microwave?"

"As long as you unplug all the stuff pulling power from the outlets, except the refrigerator and the freezer."

Angie had another thought. "Any chance of firing up the grill you pulled in from the back patio and is still cluttering up my dining room?"

"We can roll it out here. I'll pull the garage door up enough to provide venting."

"In that case we'll upgrade the menu to hot dogs. We only have about twenty packages of those."

"I wasn't thinking of right now. It's too late to start any new projects. Can you cook something else to feed us?"

"We can manage. I need some help." Angie took Sandy and Amy by the arms. "Come along ladies, let's see if we can rustle something up."

Aaron nodded. "Great. See if Molly is able to help and send Mike out here."

Amy followed Angie back to the kitchen. Mike and Molly Barker were waiting for them. Mike smiled and patted a dry t-shirt. "I sure am glad to be dry and out of the rain. It seems like forever since this nightmare started. We can't thank you enough."

Molly was sitting in a chair at the kitchen table, sobbing into a towel.

Amy saw the terror gripping the poor woman. She put an arm around her shoulder.

Molly looked up at her with red eyes and groaned. "This is horrible, horrible. Everything I had is gone."

Amy hugged Molly. "I sure know how you feel. We had to drive up here from Punta Gorda. My home is gone too. All of us are as beat up and rattled as you. Up until now it's me who's been losing it. Guess the two of us are going to have to stick together."

Molly rubbed her eyes with the towel and looked up again. "What's your name?"

"I'm Amy." She smiled and nodded her head.

Molly smiled back a little and took Amy's hand. "Besides losing everything we own; the worst part was being alone. It's better having people like you around."

"I wouldn't put me down as a great role model. I'm scared out of my skin too."

Angie smiled and walked over to hug both women. "The

four of us need to get busy and fix something to eat. Somewhere around here I have a recipe book for cooking in a microwave. It's about the only thing still working."

Molly stared around the room. "How come you still have power?"

Amy helped Molly to her feet. "We have a generator. You must be hungry. If you can help, it'll go faster."

"I'm happy to do whatever you need."

"That's great. Between the two of us we almost make a whole person."

Molly grunted and dried her hair with the towel. "Okay, partial person, what do we do?"

Angie had the answer. "There're paper plates and plastic knives, forks and spoons in that cabinet over there. By the way, Mike, Aaron wants you to join the others in the garage."

"Fine. I wouldn't be much help in here anyway. I'll go see what I can do to lend a hand."

Night fell by the time the women finished making the meal. Angie dusted off her hands. "Molly can you step out to the garage and tell the men we're ready to eat?"

When she went out the door, Angie turned back to Amy. "That was a very good thing you did getting Molly settled down. You got through to her better than I could."

"The look in her eyes is the way I feel in my gut. I felt sorry for her and wanted her to know she wasn't the only one whose world has been washed away."

Angie looked into the living room. Rain pounded like a drum on the roof of the tent. "I hope we don't get washed away. Anyway, don't get to thinking this is all too big for us to handle. It's big, but it still depends on what each of us does."

Amy realized this was the best she'd felt in two days. "I believe that. I'm sorry it took me so long to stop being a burden."

"You're doing fine."

❖

The kitchen door opened and the four men came streaming in. Aaron lifted his nose and took a big breath. "Something smells awfully good."

Angie hugged her husband. "I don't know how good it is but there's plenty. Get a couple chairs from the laundry room to put around the table."

The eight found a place around the kitchen table. The bowls of food went around, plates were filled, and very little conversation went on while everyone eagerly ate.

Aaron wiped his mouth with a napkin and pushed his empty plate aside. The other plates were equally empty. "That was good. I didn't realize how hungry I was."

Angie got up and started picking up the dishes. "We've haven't had a meal since breakfast very early in the morning yesterday."

With a small belch Aaron went on. "Since then we've gone through a hurricane, had our roof ripped off, and gotten beaten to pieces. For certain, there are more crappy and dangerous things to come, but we've stabilized our situation and are safe for the moment. Certainly, more bad things are coming, and we'll have to make a lot of tough choices. However, I think we need to get some sleep before we start making them."

He looked across the table at Mike and Molly. "You two have got to be worn out."

Mike nodded. "That's for sure. Point me to a flat place to lay down."

"As we agreed, we need to keep a watch, both for any other people who might find us, and to sound the alarm if something else awful happens. I'll take the first watch. The rest of you can turn in."

One by one, the others went off to sleep.

Aaron sat alone in the kitchen and lowered his head in deep thought.

Chapter 14
Thinking Ahead

<u>Tuesday night</u>

Aaron listened as the heavy rain roared on the tent. It wasn't quite the peace and quiet he wanted. The kitchen wasn't much less noisy. He picked up a lantern and headed for the garage, pausing to look inside the tent. Not a soul was awake.

The garage was hot and humid, but quieter. Aaron opened a chair and sat down. Up until now, he thought, they were lucky. Surviving the hurricane was a miracle, nobody got killed, and part of the house was still intact. What he needed most now was any kind of word on conditions around him. Talking to someone would ease his mind.

He pulled his hand-set radio out of the case on his hip, tuned to the emergency channel handling traffic from people like him, and turned up the volume. There was still a lot of cross talk transmissions overlapping each other. The operator on the other end was trying to keep order, constantly telling people to wait their turn. He was even giving numbers to survivors saying he would talk to everyone one at a time, and to stay off the radio, so he could.

With a pause in other cross talk, Aaron keyed the transmit button. "I need a number."

It took him three times to send those four words.

Finally, the operator responded. "Okay that makes eight, counting the man who just called. I'm going to start talking to people. When you hear your number, start talking. Until I get to you, everybody stay off the radio."

Aaron supposed the guy was talking to him, so he sat and listened.

Over the next hour, Aaron heard desperate people describing the situation they were facing and asking for help. There was still cross talk, but the man on the other end could hear what people were saying. Nowhere in the exchanges did the operator say anything about any aid. He seemed to be collecting information. Aaron sat on the back of the golf cart and made a list of things to do while he waited his turn.

"Very well, thank you, number seven," said the operator. "Go ahead number eight."

"I'm Aaron Colson. I live in Harmony village. "There are eight people in my home. None of us seriously injured by the hurricane. We lost most of our roof. The kitchen and garage are still covered. I have minimum power and, for the moment, we are stable."

There was a pause before the operator came back. "Where are you on the hill?"

"Right at the top."

"That puts you in the same place as the other people who withstood the hurricane and have made their way to higher ground."

"How bad is it?"

"What used to be The Villages, is now a city of islands. Yours is one of them."

"What have you heard about how much longer this rain will last?"

"Don't know, exactly. All night and through tomorrow for sure, according to the people watching in the command center."

"I figured as much."

"Central Florida is flooded. Here in The Villages that includes most of the Rec. Centers. When this started, the people in charge around here watched the coverage on the Weather Channel. When they started talking about two hurricanes hitting both coasts at the same time, our command center bypassed all other contingencies and went right to catastrophe planning. They hit the red button. Calls went out to every emergency center they could contact, asking for immediate help. That help is on the way from all over the country, but most of it hasn't been able to get through. We now have thousands of people crammed into the Rec centers we have left and other places not yet flooded."

"The water is coming up my hill. How long before if spills through my front door?"

"The best estimates we have right now is that the water is rising about a foot an hour. Where does that put you?"

"I've not looked. It's too dark to make guesses."

When he finished, the operator came back. "You're in better shape than most, and you only have eight to worry about. Right now, we've been able to divert a few helicopters to hill tops and rescue people who don't have any more choices. I'm really sorry, pal, more important issues come first. It looks like you are on your own, at least for another day."

Aaron bubbled his lips in a little snort. "Not even one boat with some necessities?"

"We have boats. The problem is trying navigate through all the floating junk. We've already lost two boats and four men. I couldn't ask them to make a long run trying to get to you."

Aaron pushed away the anger. None of this was the operator's fault. He tried to keep his voice calm. "I understand. How do I contact you again?"

"Two of us are manning this frequency. We're both getting as much information as we can and talking to people like you. I'm going to get some sleep now. I'll be back about four a.m. I've added your name to my list. You're number eight. When you listen, wait your turn. I'm Scott. Say it's you calling me. I've written down everything you told me, so only tell me what's changed."

Aaron looked at his watch—it was past ten p.m. "Roger that, Scott. I'll call again at four."

Knowing more about what was going on around him, made Aaron feel better. Especially since he'd made a contact he could speak to later. He put the radio away and held up a lantern to see better. It was still too dark. He turned on two more lanterns.

His oversized garage would be where they would do most of their living, sleeping and eating. For the moment, he could reserve the tent as a place for the women to sleep. If more survivors found them, there could be injured people and the tent would be used as an aid and treatment center. He made a mental note to discuss it with Ben. He would need a quiet place, away from the commotion of the garage to work without any distractions.

In any case, preparing the garage was still the first-priority. Beads of sweat dripped from his forehead. He grabbed a shop towel and wiped his face and neck. Until today, the garage was only a garage, filled with his gardening tools, storage and overflow from the house. Now its new purpose made Aaron look at it with different eyes. It was like one of those images you see in a magazine. If you stare at it long enough, it turns into a different picture.

There were two doors for vehicles in the garage. One was the big one to park two cars, and the other for the much smaller golf cart. Aaron wondered if he could open the little door without getting flooded. He walked over, pulled the latch cord, and inched the door up. Very little water came in. He raised the door a little more and leaned over to peek under it. A refreshing stream of air flowed in.

That'll be cooler for everyone.

As he thought, most of the rain was blowing away from his north-facing house and the roof eaves made a two-foot semi-dry area in front of the door. He pulled the door open completely and looked out. It was too dark to see much. The nearby houses across the street made the scene look like a bombed-out city. Aaron shook his head in despair for his neighbors who had died in the hurricane. Ben said he found nine bodies. Aaron couldn't even see the bodies of the couple he'd said were lying in the street. They were too far down the hill.

He looked closer at his own yard. The light of the lantern

he'd hung on his lamp post was still blinking as a beacon for anyone looking for safety and shelter.

On an impulse, Arron rummaged through one of the cabinets and found an aerosol can fitted with a little horn. There were a couple others as well. He stuck the can to the outside and pushed the button. A loud honk sounded.

Angie awoke to the sound of the horn.

What's Aaron up to now?

She got up and slipped out of the tent. Nobody else stirred from the noise. As she opened the door to the garage, an invigorating draft of cool air rushed across her face with Aaron right behind it. "Did the toot from the horn wake you?"

"I'm the only one. What are you doing?"

"I lifted the golf cart garage door."

"No kidding? Any rain getting inside?"

"Hardly any. We're facing away from the storm. Come see for yourself."

Angie stepped into the garage and took a deep breath. "It's refreshing."

"I got through to somebody on the radio."

"Who was it?"

"A guy named Scott. I think he's working out of an improvised command center."

"What's the latest?"

"Major flooding across all The Villages. People who made it through the hurricane are gathering in rec centers on higher ground."

"Can we do that?" Angie knew the answer before she asked the question from the frightful look on her husband's face.

"Nope. We're on higher ground but it's surrounded by flood waters."

The shadow of claustrophobia washed through her mind as she turned her face aside for long seconds.

Angie turned back to Aaron, took a deep breath, and spoke her worst fear. "Nobody's coming, are they?"

Aaron's features softened at once. He smiled and put an arm around her. "Scott said we're in better shape than most. We are."

Angie's pent-up frustration came pouring out. "This is bullshit. Everything we do is so goddamned hard."

"Yeah, but I think this is the last place the storm will reach. Every hour we can hold things together, the closer we are to the hurricanes moving north."

"How many hours?"

"I'm hoping no longer than thirty."

"Look what we've been through the last thirty hours."

Aaron nodded his head. "I know, but we have to go on."

"How about a little more of that cool breeze?"

The two stepped outside the cart door, under the eaves, and stared at the gloom of the storm. The devastation around them was heart breaking.

Aaron pointed at the mountain of debris floating in the water down the hill. Piles of trees, broken parts of buildings, furniture, and, presumably, humans were in the wreckage.

Angie didn't want to add to her husband's problems. "It sure is a mess out there. Did your guy on the radio talk about the water rising up the hill?"

"Not much."

He's not saying something.

Angie decided to change the subject. She pointed at the can on the back of the golf cart. "Is that the gizmo making the honk?"

"Yeah, I got a couple more cans of it. I hope it helps people find us."

"It woke me up."

"Anybody else?"

"Not a soul as far as I could tell. Everybody is dead to the world. We all need sleep."

"What about you, my sweet little wife? You need rest as much as anyone."

"I'm your relief for the next watch."

"That's not for a couple more hours. You ought to go back to sleep."

"I'm in charge of making sure the one who needs rest the most, gets it."

"I'm all right."

"Why sure you are. You've got a knot on the side of your head the size of a golf ball."

"I'm okay."

"Your hands are shaking worse than Amy's."

"I was sort of hoping it didn't show."

"It probably doesn't to anyone but me. At least so far. But it will, if you keep on charging ahead like this."

"Ahh, Angie."

"Don't Ahh Angie me, mister. In case you haven't figured it out, the people asleep in the tent are counting on you to do the right thing and lead them through this. I've no idea what we'd do if you lost it."

"Ahh, Angie."

"You're only allowed one of those a day—or night. Now how about you taking advantage of this nice cool breeze and getting some rest? I'll guard the door and watch for anybody."

Aaron stuck the can out the door and gave it a long toot. "We ought to do this every hour. People who hear it will know somebody is doing something besides tread water."

"The only thing I want to hear from you is snoring."

"You gotta wake me by four a.m. I'll have another chance to talk with the command center. Maybe we'll hear good news."

Chapter 15
Sanctuary

<u>Four a.m. Wednesday</u>

Angie shined her small flashlight around the tent. When she spotted Mason sleeping in a corner, she crept over and touched him gently on the leg. Mason sat up immediately as if he wasn't sleeping at all. He rubbed his eyes and looked at her. She cocked her head, and he followed her out to the garage.

"So that's where the cool air is coming from." Mason pointed at the open golf cart door. "I felt it a few hours ago. Sure did make it easier to sleep."

"I didn't think you were asleep. You got up so fast."

"It's a conditioned response. Whenever you're in a tough or dangerous situation, you sleep with one eye open."

"Did you get any sleep?"

"Oh, sure. You grab snoozes whenever you can."

"Before I sent him off to sleep, Aaron talked to somebody on the radio. I guess all he heard was it'll keep raining and nobody is coming to help us."

Angie relayed as much of the conversation she could remember. When she finished, she waved at the open golf cart door. "Aaron pulled up the door during his watch. He was looking for a way to empty out this garage to make way for more survivors."

"The cool air feels good. How long has Aaron been asleep?"

"I got him down about eleven. He made me promise to wake him, right now—four a.m.—so he could talk to the guy, Scott, again. Aaron said we were number eight."

"Where's the radio?"

"In the kitchen. I plugged it in to recharge the battery."

"Let's see what they're saying before we wake Aaron."

Mason went to the kitchen and brought back the radio. He turned it on and held it so Angie could hear.

A voice was speaking. "...mmand center. Previously contacted survivor centers should report status by the numbers given you. Number one."

Angie and Mason listened to another stranded group. They talked about minimal shelter, dwindling supplies, and rising water effecting a growing number of people. It took five minutes for them to transmit everything.

Mason looked at his watch. "At this rate, it'll be awhile before they get to us. Let Aaron sleep."

"Glad to hear that. He was drooping." Angie picked up the horn can, stuck it out the golf cart door, and gave it a healthy honk. "Aaron said we should blow this horn every hour."

"What else did he say?"

"He wrote a long to-do list."

"Let's see it."

Mason read the list, stopping to have Angie translate Aaron's scribbles. "Most of the things on this list have to do with clearing out the garage." He looked at his watch again. "I'll need some help with that, but we can let everybody sleep. Sun-up won't come for another couple of hours. There won't be much light, but enough for us to work. With the grill out here, I can fix something to eat."

"I'll get Sandy up. She can help."

"Go get started. I'm going through this list again."

Mason had settled on the golf cart when Angie came back to the garage.

She walked over and took Mason's arm. "The power's out on the refrigerator."

"The generator. Hope it's only out of gas. I'll go check." He got up, started toward the open door, then stopped and turned back to Angie. "We don't want to miss the command center calling our number. Go back to the kitchen and listen for it."

"If our power's been out, we didn't get a charge on the radio. How did we get a signal?"

"Aaron turned it off before he went to sleep. There was enough juice left to make it work. If I can get the generator running, we'll charge it up."

Angie went back to the kitchen. Mason pulled his coverall off a hook on a wall in the garage, put it on, and zipped it up. Then he stepped out the garage door, hugging the eaves of the roof along the side of the garage to stay mostly out of the rain. When he got to the generator, Mason pulled a palm frond off the metal awning above it. The machine was not running. Four five-gallon gas containers sat next to it. Mason jiggled them, two were empty. He picked up a full can and filled the generator's tank. He punched the choke a couple times and pushed the starter. The generator surged to life.

Gotta find more gas today, or we're screwed.

When he rounded the corner of the garage, Mason saw the lights of two vehicles through the rain. He watched as they meandered through the debris on the streets and lawns. As they got closer, Mason could see they were two golf carts. He ran out into the rain and waved his arms. It was still too dark for anyone to see him. He ducked back into the garage and grabbed the horn can. He carried it back outside, pointed it in the direction of the lights, and gave a long toot.

The lights on the golf carts now shined directly at him. Mason stood on the driveway and waved his arms again. A moment later the golf carts pulled up to the front of the garage.

A man jumped from the cart. "My wife is hurt. Is there anything you can do to help?"

Mason looked into the golf cart at a woman clearly in pain. "We've got a doc. Let's get her inside."

By this time, both carts were empty. Counting the injured woman, there were six people in this group. Mason helped the man get his wife out of the cart, and everyone stepped into the dry garage. She slumped down on a chair, her face white with pain.

Angie ran into the garage. Sandy was right behind her.

Mason turned to them. "I don't know how they got here, but we've got six more people. This woman needs medical aid. One of you go wake Ben."

Angie dashed back inside. Sandy smirked at her husband. "Can't leave you alone for a minute." She turned to the group, dripping water from soaked clothing. "We haven't got much, but you're welcome to all we have."

The injured woman grimaced in pain, leaning heavily back on the chair.

Her husband kept his arm on her shoulder. "What you've got is a whole bunch more than we've had. Finding someone else in this mess makes me feel better."

Ben came into the garage, wiping the sleep from his eyes. "Who needs medical help?"

"We do. Or at least my wife does."

Amy came through the door, trying to smooth her hair. She ran to the injured woman. "You're gonna be okay. My husband is the best doc. Let me help you inside." She and Ben supported the woman, and they disappeared into the house.

Angie stepped out of the kitchen. "Mason, the guy on the radio called for number six."

"Shit. Everything's happening at once. You better wake Aaron."

"I think he's stirring. All the people coming and going from the tent has everyone half-awake. Now we have power again, we can use the microwave and refrigerator."

Mason looked around at the frightened newcomers. "It's a good thing. No telling when any of these people last ate."

This got the attention of one of the men in the new group. "We've been hiding under the part of our roof that wasn't blown away. I'm starving."

Angie stepped over and put her hand on the man's arm. "Breakfast is the next thing on our agenda. How about a hand hauling the grill out here?"

"Show me the way, Ma'am."

"I can help," said another man.

The three of them went back into the house. Shortly the men returned, hauling the grill into the garage next to the golf cart. One of them opened the valve on the propane tank and turned the knobs on the grill. It came to life.

Aaron sensed the activity around him. He turned and sat up. A vigorous massage of his face with both hands helped him shake the sleep away, grimacing in pain as he bumped the gash on the side of his head. He looked around. Ben and Amy were working on a woman under the light of a lantern. He realized someone had found them in the storm.

As he climbed to his feet, Angie came into the tent. "You gotta get to the radio."

"Are they calling us?"

"Not yet, but they're up to number six."

Aaron followed Angie into the kitchen. He picked up the radio. "We still have power?"

"We didn't until an hour ago. The generator quit. Mason filled the tank and turned it back on."

"I knew it would run out of gas while we slept. That was the one time we didn't need power."

He glanced at his watch. "It's after five. Why didn't you wake me?"

"I got Mason up at the end of my watch. He turned on the radio and heard them starting through the numbers. We figured you could sleep a little longer."

"Thanks for that. How many new people do we have?"

"Six, counting the hurt lady. I had a couple of the men haul the grill out to the garage, next to the golf cart. I was starting to make something hot to eat."

"So, now we've got fourteen people. How much longer will the food hold out?"

"Not very long. After today, we'll be down to figuring out how to put together a meal using the stuff in cans."

The radio crackled to life. "Roger, six, we're doing all we can. Number seven."

There was no response. The operator tried again. "Calling number seven. Do you read me over?"

Still silence. Aaron hugged Angie. "A lot of things could have happened to keep them from calling in."

"Including them being flooded out, or worse."

"Calling number seven. Do you read, over?"

Aaron and Angie stared at the radio, as the operator tried several more times to get a response.

As they listened, Ben came into the kitchen. "The woman you brought in has a dislocated shoulder and a compound fracture of her arm above the wrist. I relocated her shoulder and put a splint on her arm. Her condition is critical.

Aaron sounded surprised. "From a broken arm?"

"Besides the broken arm, the woman is in shock, exhausted, dehydrated, and probably hasn't eaten in the past day. I started a saline IV, boosted it with antibiotics, and gave her a shot for pain. We need to move her to a place where she can get better care than I can do here."

Scott was back on the radio "Okay. I'm going to move on. Number eight."

Aaron snatched the radio and keyed the mike. "This is Aaron, calling Scott, over."

"Roger, Aaron. What's your situation?"

"We took in eight more survivors overnight bringing us up to fourteen. One of them is an injured woman. Our doc says her condition is critical. She needs to be evacuated."

"Roger, I understand. Conditions overnight have gotten worse. Most of the few helicopters we've seen are only bringing in food, water, medical supplies and evacuating our injured. The rising water is flooding the hills. Small groups of people retreated to the tops of those hills and the choppers are pulling them out before they drown. We can't reach you."

Ben and Angie watched as Aaron pushed the transmit key again. "Roger. Not good news. Any word on how much longer this rain will last?"

"The guys in the command center say to expect it to rain all day and into the night. After that, they say the storms will move north, and we might dry out a little."

Aaron glanced at his watch. "Sunup is about an hour away. When it gets lighter, I'll be able to see how far up our hill the water has risen. We could be in big trouble. When can I call you back?"

"When I finish talking to people on my list, we'll listen for other survivor groups I've not spoken to. Then we'll start over. You are still number eight, Aaron. Be ready when it comes your turn. I'm hoping to speak to people every hour or so."

"Roger, Scott. We'll be listening."

Mason came back to the kitchen as Aaron finished. "I heard the last of that. We won't have power long if we don't find some gas for the generator. The battery on that two-way radio will last awhile, but if we don't recharge it, we could be without communications."

Aaron slumped back against the kitchen counter. He put his hand around his chin as he thought. "We can't go looking for gas or anything until it gets lighter. Until then, we can start cleaning out the unnecessary things in the garage, starting with the golf cart. We need room to do some cooking. How many able-bodied people do we have?"

Angie sat down some bowls and plates she had taken from the cupboard. "There are the two guys who hauled the grill to the garage."

"I think the three of us can manage." He gave Mason an appraising look. "You should lay off on all this heavy work." He turned to Ben. "You should stay with your injured lady. Is anybody with her now?"

"Amy got up with me when they brought her in. She's looking after her."

That got Aaron's attention. "How's your wife doing?"

"Better. She talked to Mason. Whatever he said is helping keep her emotions under control. Now, helping me is letting her concentrate on other things."

Angie pushed her husband's arm. "We still have to eat. Sandy can help me. Maybe Molly can give us a hand as well. We have a full bottle of propane?"

"As much as we'll use it, we'll need more pretty soon. Add propane to the list of things to look for when we start moving around this morning."

Mason peeked around the corner and into the dark tent. "You said the six of us were gonna get stretched thin to take care of other people. Looks like that's the way it is."

Aaron scrunched his face in agreement. "We'll let as many who can, keep sleeping."

Chapter 16
Hard Reality

<u>**Seven a.m. Wednesday**</u>

Aaron stepped into the garage. Two men were sitting in the golf cart. "I guess you heard what we were talking about in the kitchen. We need something to eat. After that, we'll get everyone together, and I'll tell them everything I know about our situation. First, we need to get this golf cart out, so there's room to cook." One of the men looked around. "Where you going to put it?"

"Outside."

"In this rain?"

Aaron walked over and pulled a tarp off a pile. "I'm going to park it as close to the big garage door as I can, and then cover it." The other man looked at Aaron sharply. "I'm starting to dry out from being soaked for two days. I don't mean to be a wimp or look unhelpful, but I wish there was a way to do this without getting wet, again."

"I have waterproof coveralls. Not enough for everyone. We'll reserve our supply for those of us working outside." Aaron walked over to a wall where the coveralls hung and handed one to each of the others. He pulled on his own coveralls. "Let's go." Aaron backed his golf cart out of the garage. He parked it as close to the big garage door as possible. The eaves kept most of the water from splashing on the cart. He directed traffic as they eased another of the carts right behind his. Aaron shouted over the rain. "That other cart won't fit here. It would block the entryway to the front door. Drive it next to the others. This tarp is big enough to cover most of them." The three of them threw the cover over the carts, and secured it with some bags of dirt. When they finished, the men stepped back inside, stomping their feet and running their hands down the coveralls to shed the water. One man slipped the hood off his head. "It's good to be able to go outside and not get drenched.

Aaron looked at the wet floor. "It won't stay dry in here very long with traffic coming and going through this door, but we still have to clear out space enough for us to make breakfast."

Mason watched in the kitchen door while Aaron and the others moved the golf carts, and carried tools and boxes out the golf cart door. He was glad he didn't need to give Aaron a hand. The wounds in his hip and butt burned like fire. The beating he took, and the heavy work putting up the tent aggravated the injury. Later, he could ask Ben to look at it and change the dressing. Right now, he would take the lead preparing a meal.

Angie must have read his mind. She came up and took his arm. "You're a better cook than me. Especially when you're feeding a crowd, like at your restaurant. Has Aaron cleared out space enough to get around the grill and make a serving area?"

"Looks like. I need to set up a couple folding tables."

"They're right over there, against the wall. You put them up while I get things out."

Mason stood aside as Aaron swept the excess water off the floor with a broom and lay down a dry tarp.

It took Mason a few minutes to unfold the tables and line them up next to the grill. He turned back to Aaron. "That's all the set-up we need. I'm going to go look at our food supply and start cooking."

Mason went back to the kitchen and pulled open the refrigerator door. "This was shut all night, so even without power, it held in most of the cold."

Sandy looked over her shoulder. "Looks like nothing's spoiled." "Maybe in the refrigerator, but the freezer section won't stay frozen if we keep turning the generator off and on." Angie listened to the two as she continued taking things from the cupboards. "The big freezer will stay colder, longer. We can move some stuff there." She pushed past the two and took out eggs, bacon, packages of hash brown potatoes and slammed the door. "All of a sudden we have a lot of people to feed. You guys know more about that than any of us. After all, you have a restaurant."

Sandy slumped down onto a dining room chair. Tears filled her eyes. "Had a restaurant. I hadn't thought much about it until now. Our home, the restaurant—everything we own, are gone."

The despair on her daughter's face caused Angie to walk over and bend down to hug her. "I'm sorry, honey. I know this is hard."

Mason joined them. "Yeah, sweetie, I'm sorry too."

Sandy stood up and slumped into her husband's chest. He put his arms around her, and they shared a long embrace.

Finally, Mason stepped back and raised an eyebrow. "Even with all these shitty things, and more shitty stuff ahead, we still have to cook breakfast."

A voice spoke behind them. "I wish I had better news."

Mason turned to a grim-faced Ben. "What's the latest on your patient?"

Ben looked around, then pushed the others into a corner. He half whispered. "Not good. I've done all I can for her and it's not enough. I don't even have any oxygen. Her husband is with her now. I think I'm gonna lose her."

Mason shook his head sadly. "I'm sure you've done all you can, Doc. Sometimes people slip away, no matter what you do."

"True enough. It never makes it easier."

Angie put a hand on Ben's arm. "Where's Amy?"

"Still with her. She's been talking to the woman since she came in. I wish I had a dozen nurses like her."

Angie smiled. "She found something to do besides wallow in the past?"

"That's right. I've seen it before. People turn away from their own troubles when they have to think about a bigger crisis."

"Go back and tell her she needs a break. Send her out here. We'll help her catch her breath and have a cup of coffee."

"The tent is hot and humid. Any way to make it better?"

Mason spoke up. "I'll talk to Aaron. We'll see what we can

do."

Ben nodded and turned, leaving without another word.

Mason walked over to the main kitchen counter and looked at the food Angie put out. "This isn't going to be enough to feed everyone."

Angie joined him. "What else do we need?"

"I suppose these are all the eggs you have?"

"Yeah, two dozen. I don't keep much more than that. Those should be enough to make a breakfast."

"You need eggs to make other things. We ought to save them for that. Do you have any pasta?"

"A whole drawer full."

"Pasta has lots of carbohydrates. Exactly what everyone needs. It's very filling. We should put a big pot of water on the grill and start cooking pasta in bulk. You can set it aside for more meals. Heat it up in the microwave."

"For as long as the power lasts."

"Let me worry about that. As soon as it gets light, we'll go out and do some exploring."

Aaron came back to the kitchen. The men who'd helped in the garage were right behind him. Both stepped into the tent to lay down and rest next to their wives.

Aaron looked at the bowls, dishes, and food on the counter. "Are the rest of you as hungry as I am?"

Mason was pouring water into a metal pot. "Give Mom and I a chance to sort out our food supply. Then I'll start cooking. I think we're all hungry."

"Great. What's for breakfast?"

"Nothing very familiar. We don't have enough for scrambled eggs, or enough bread for toast. But we have enough bacon for about three slices apiece, plenty of tortillas, hash browns and lots and lots of pasta."

"Heavens, what a concoction. Well, do the best you can."

Angie and Sandy followed Mason into the garage, loaded down with armfuls of ingredients. He lit the grill and looked at his cooking area. In addition to the open side, there was a flat grill. Mason dumped two pounds of bacon on that side, separating slices as the grill heated. He put the metal pot on the other side and started the water boiling. "How are we fixed for pancake mix?"

"I've got a lot of that."

"Good, put a few eggs in that mix. Have any milk left that's not spoiled?"

Angie headed back to the kitchen. "I'll look. How big a batch should I mix?"

"Enough for about two dozen big flapjacks."

"Coming up."

In short order, Mason had food cooking all over the grill and the smell of food filled the garage. Aaron stood in the kitchen door savoring the aroma. "How much longer?"

"You can wake everybody up. By the time they wipe the sleep from their eyes it'll be ready."

Aaron went around the corner and spoke into the tent. "Good morning. Breakfast is almost ready. Some of you haven't eaten in a while, so this will be a good way to start the day. Afterward, we'll have a meeting and I'll tell you all I know about our current situation and what we must do to take care of each other."

The sound of stirring with grumbles and groans was a signal people were waking. Aaron went to the far corner where Ben was treating the injured woman. Her husband knelt at her side, holding her hand, and speaking softly to her. Amy looked up at Aaron. He cocked his head at her, motioning for her to join the others. Ben said something to her. She nodded, got up and came to the kitchen. Fatigue and worry marked her face.

Angie was ready with a fresh cup of coffee. "You want something in this, honey?"

"I use a creamer, if we have any."

"We do. Aaron likes it in his coffee, and so far it hasn't gone bad." Angie opened the refrigerator, took out a bottle, and poured some in Amy's cup.

Amy took a couple of sips, then put her head back on her shoulder and then back and forth to work out the kinks. "That's good, thanks."

Before they could finish their conversation, people emerged from the tent. Molly came in with Mike. She took her cup of coffee and put an arm around Amy. "I slept pretty good before the other people came in. I saw you and Ben working on that lady. How is she?"

"Not very good." She turned back to Angie. "Ben wants to know if you can make something light for her."

"I'll heat some soup in the microwave."

Aaron shook his head. "I hope that helps." He picked up a cup and poured coffee. "Since you already have the creamer out, can I have some?" He smiled down at Amy. "Us coffee connoisseurs have to stick together."

Amy leaned against Aaron a little. "You always say the right thing, at the right time, and in the right way."

"You and Ben have been up for a while. Why don't you take him a cup of coffee? I'll send in a plate of food for you both in a bit."

By this time, the two newest couples had joined Mike and Molly in the kitchen. Angie poured them coffee from a pitcher. "I've got another pot brewing, so you can have seconds."

"Breakfast," hollered Mason from the garage.

Angie pointed at the pile of paper plates and plastic utensils on the counter. "Get yourself a plate and a fork. Have Mason fill 'em up. Then come back and take a seat around the table.

Aaron followed them. Mason had pancakes and bacon ready. He served them onto the eagerly offered plates. Aaron waited for everyone to take their food back to the kitchen, then picked up a couple plates. "This is for Amy and Ben. I'll see if the husband of the hurt lady wants to eat."

Mason filled them up and Aaron took them inside to the tent.

Ben looked up when Aaron stooped down next to them and handed each a plate. He touched the husband on the shoulder. "Why don't you go have breakfast?"

"I'm not hungry."

Ben stared into the man's eyes. "You need a break, and Aaron will tell us what he heard on the radio. Get something to eat and have a cup of coffee. I'll call you if there's any change."

Aaron helped the man to his feet. "Come on along and join the rest of us."

The man followed Aaron to the kitchen, and a place made for him around the table. Angie set a fresh cup of coffee in front of him.

The others tried to console him. None of them asked about his wife. They all knew the situation. Soon, the table grew quiet as people concentrated on eating.

Aaron nodded in satisfaction and motioned the family to the garage. He closed the door to the kitchen. Mason served them, and they sat down, balancing plates on their knees.

While they ate, Aaron summed up the facts. "These new people are in shock and overwhelmed by the situation. They probably think they've found a safe place. We know that's not the case. All we've done is stabilize our shelter at a pretty low level. That could change at any moment, and we could all be fighting to stay alive."

Mason wiped his hands on an apron and picked up a plate. "Having something to eat will help, but it won't take them long to remember how miserable they are."

"Right. That's why we need to keep everyone busy and their minds off their troubles. As soon as it gets light, there's a lot to do."

Sandy rolled a forkful of pasta. "The last six who came in, have only had a couple hours of sleep. None for the man with the injured wife. They're all older people. We can't expect much from them."

"Which is why we'll get them busy reorganizing our sleeping areas. I'll tell them the faster we can do that, the sooner they can get some rest." Aaron said no more, turning his attention to eating. The others did the same.

When he finished, Mason got up and crumpled his plate, throwing it into the trash can. "Whoever is left in the tent will be more comfortable if we can open more of it and let the cooler air come in."

Aaron nodded. "We can do that, at least with the opening facing the front door. I don't think we can do more if we expect the tent to stay dry."

"Are you going to move the men out here, and leave the tent for the women?"

"Now's the time, especially with Ben staying with the hurt lady."

Angie walked over to a pair of louvered room dividers leaning against a wall. "We can put these up on two sides away from the corner of the garage. It will afford the men a little privacy. Where are those air mattresses?"

"I'll find them. They're in one of those cubicles."

More light filled the room through the open golf cart door. The sun had risen beyond the banks of heavy clouds which filled the sky. The relentless rain continued to fall.

"Sunup," announced Aaron. "It's time to get everyone together and tell them what needs to be done."

Chapter 17
Searching the Neighborhood

<u>Sunrise, Wednesday</u>

Aaron led his wife, along with Mason and Sandy, back to the kitchen. The newest survivors sat quietly at the table.

The man with the injured wife looked up at Aaron. "I'm Simon Fraser. I appreciate you giving us shelter and food. Never thought I'd have pasta for breakfast. I need to get back to Cheri, but you said you were going to give us an update on the situation."

"Right. Here's what I know. I've been talking to The Villages command center on the radio. It's going to keep raining today and through the night before these hurricanes begin moving north. There's widespread flooding over central Florida. Only the tops of the hills, like the one we're on, is above water. There's no way they can evacuate us, so we're on our own.

"Mason and I are going out to look for fuel and propane for the grill. What we have won't last for more than a few hours."

One of the men, a neighbor of Aaron's, spoke up. "I have two, five-gallon cans of gas in my garage. Don't know about the propane tank though."

"We'll take a look. Anybody else?"

The people at the table looked around at each other. Nobody spoke.

"Okay. While we're gone, help empty the garage to make room for the men to rest. We'll keep the tent for the women and Cheri. We might find others needing medical help. Angie will tell you what to do."

One woman's voice rose above the murmurs. "Whew—I'm so tired I can't think. Of course, we'll help. We can't thank you enough for your help, and we appreciate the shelter and the big meal. You guys are lifesavers."

Aaron leaned back against the counter. "This is hard on us all. If we pitch in together, we can finish quickly. Then you can lay down and get some real sleep."

Angie walked around the table collecting the paper plates throwing them in a trash bag. She looked out the window at the endless rain. "The sun must be up, you can't see it, but it's getting lighter."

"Not much," commented one of the women.

Aaron waved an arm around the room. "Like in here. Even with all our lanterns in the kitchen, it still seems dark. We're used to a lot more. Outside there are street lights, lights on our lamp posts and garages, and light coming from other houses. With no power, that's gone."

The woman lowered her head. "It's unnerving and scary."

"Of course, it is. So little of our normal lives remains, it would scare anyone." Aaron paused long enough to see everyone waiting for him to say something more. "We've survived a major hurricane—barely. From this point on, we must do everything we can to keep things from getting worse."

Another of the men sat up straighter. "Will it get worse?"

"Ask me that in a couple of hours."

Aaron and Mason went to the garage and put on coveralls. Mason stepped outside and pulled the cart up to the open garage door. Angie handed Aaron a plastic trash bag, with more bags in it and a wooden orange crate. He carried them to the cart, as Mason ran back into the house.

Aaron raised his voice over the rain. "Hold down the fort, honey. I've no idea what we'll find. This first trip will be short, only enough to drive around and get a better picture of what's going on."

"What if Scott calls from the command center?"

"Listen to the radio in case he does. Tell him what we're doing."

"I'll get help clearing out the garage."

"Where's my horn can?"

"Here's something better." Angie pulled a whistle from her

pocket. "Use this. The sound may not carry as far, but it won't run out of air unless you quit breathing."

"Not planning on that."

As they spoke, Mason hobbled out the door with something wrapped in a towel. He eased into the driver's seat and zipped the side curtain shut. "Ready to go?"

Aaron zipped down his curtain. "Are you ready? You're limping pretty bad."

"Yeah. It's slowing me down, but these were flesh wounds, and Doc got most everything out before he stitched me up. I'll be okay. Let me do the driving. You do the getting in and out."

"Hope it's that easy."

Mason stepped on the gas pedal, turning the wheel, so the golf cart went down the driveway and into the street. There was so much wreckage and debris littering the area, he had to pick his way through it, driving back and forth on lawns and open places in the street. It was a rough ride.

Angie and Sandy watched from the door as their men drove away.

Sandy shook her head. "Mason never complains, so I don't know how much his injuries bother him. I hope they don't run into something unexpected."

Angie hugged her daughter. "Let's stay busy till they get back." She turned to the others. "Give me a hand pulling this grill and tables away from the garage door, so we can get rid of a lot of this stuff and give ourselves more room."

Mike waved at two of the other men, and they helped him move the grill and tables. He came back to Angie when they finished. "I guess you want to take all the gardening tools and supplies outside. Aaron has enough of them."

"It'll give us more room, and we can hang wet clothes on the hangars on the tool board. You guys can put on coveralls so you don't get drenched going in and out. Take down that utility wagon hanging on the board to make it easier."

Sandy helped her mother make a large open space to the left of the door to the kitchen. Then they dragged the louvered room dividers to the wide corner and set them up to make a private square. Angie pulled air mattresses from a bin and began blowing them up with a tire pump. Sandy went across the garage and pulled out a pile of dry blankets. In the winter, her parents used them to cover plants from the frost. Now they went on the floor and over the air mattresses to give men a softer place to lay.

When they finished, Angie walked to the open garage door where men hauled the wagon, in and out of the rain. The women were helping to load for each trip.

Angie nodded her head in satisfaction. "That makes a big difference. Now we'll have more room to cook and serve food."

Mike pointed at the grill. "You want us to set this back near the door and put the folding tables up again?"

"Let's see if Aaron and Mason bring anything back."

"Well then, I guess we're done."

"We're done too. We made a dry and snug place for you to lay down and rest."

One of the men leaned over with his hands on his knees. "I can use some of that."

Angie patted the man on the shoulder. "Thanks for the help. Hang those coveralls up to dry and find yourself a soft spot."

Mike led the way for the other two. They investigated their new bedroom.

One of the men slumped down onto an air mattress. "Not used to this kind of work, especially since I'm already so worn out, I can hardly walk." The man turned over and seemed to fall asleep immediately.

Sandy shook her head. "You girls are overready for a rest yourself. Let's head back to the tent. From now on, it's a female-only place." She led the way. Nobody said anything about Ben treating Cheri, or her husband, Simon, sitting next to her. The two women followed Sandy into the tent. Sighing, they both collapsed to the floor.

Sandy watched them relax, then stepped back to the kitchen to join Angie. "These are retired, older people. Their energy reserves must be running out."

Angie leaned against a counter. "Speak for yourself, youngster."

"Are you okay, Mom?"

"Nothing a week at a luxury resort, can't fix."

Suddenly, the radio demanded attention. "Command center to number eight. Come in, Aaron."

Angie snatched the radio off her hip. She had kept her ear tuned to the chatter coming from the speaker. "Hello, command center, this is Angie, Aaron's wife. He and my son-in-law took off on the golf cart to look for supplies and more people. What's the latest?"

"More of the same. FEMA got a couple of big Chinook helicopters in with food, water, medical supplies, fuel and some first responders to help evacuate the injured."

"Any of that coming our way?"

"Sorry, it barely made a dent in the mess we have. At least everybody got something to eat and drink. We have a lot of injured people."

"When Aaron and Mason get back, I'll have him call you. No telling what he's found."

"Roger, out."

Aaron hung onto the handle above his shoulder as Mason skirted a downed palm tree.

He looked at the wrapped towel next to him. "What's that?"

"I brought my gun."

"What for?"

"Look around, Aaron. There are rats, snakes, coyotes, critters of all kinds, scrambling everywhere. They're scared and hungry. We might find bigger, more dangerous things crawling out of the water."

Aaron nodded and looked around. "I sure hadn't thought about that. I suppose wildlife is as disrupted by all this rain and flooding as we are."

"We could find gas cans and propane bottles floating around. That would mean going into the water to get them. Doing that is nuts."

"A propane bottle is probably hooked to a grill. We might see one near the edge of the waterline."

"We still have to be goddamned careful."

Mason started driving around the top of the hill, skirting the floodwaters. As they drove, the men got a look at the horrifying destruction which had turned a quiet neighborhood into ruins. Most of the houses had lost their roofs, and many homes obliterated. It wasn't only the devastation of smashed homes. Bodies were floating in the water.

Aaron pointed at the house where his neighbor said he had gas. The walls of the garage were still standing. "Pull over there. I'll jump out and see if anything is left."

When Mason pulled to a stop, Aaron unzipped his side curtain and jumped out. He stepped past piles of debris and picked his way into the shell of the garage. He returned shortly, a five-gallon gas can in each hand. "Look what I found."

"You be careful going into these ruined houses. Any walls still standing could collapse."

Aaron went to the back of the golf cart and turned the rear seat down to reveal a handy, flat cargo space. He set the gas cans on the cargo bed and secured them with bungee cords. "This will give us another ten hours of running time on our generator."

"No propane tank?"

"Didn't see one. People don't usually store propane in their garages." Aaron looked down the street and then pulled the whistle from his pocket and gave it a good toot. "Mom was right.

This whistle is loud enough. If anyone is around, maybe they'll run out of what shelter they have and signal us."

For the next half hour, the men drove carefully from house to house. Aaron found another can of gas.

Skirting the fringe of the wreckage and water, Aaron spotted a grill mixed in the mess. He jumped out of the cart and went to investigate. Sure enough, a propane tank was hooked to a grill. He balanced on a pile of trash and began unscrewing the tank. The water near him stirred, and then splashed. A six-foot alligator sprang from the water and snapped at him.

Aaron staggered back in shock and fright, crying out. "Mason, help."

He looked back at the golf cart. Mason was fumbling to separate the gun from the towel.

Aaron grabbed an uprooted bush, sticking it in the jaws of the alligator.

As he struggled, gunshots rang out behind him. Almost at his feet, the alligator thrashed his last breath. The water turned red for a moment. He turned and looked at Mason, who was lowering his gun.

"Told ya."

Aaron strode past Mason without a word and piled the propane tank on the cargo space, tying it down. Then he got in the cart, shaking, as Mason got in the other side.

Aaron put his arms on his knees and cupped his face in his hands. "This violence, destruction, and death are getting me down. Bad things happen right on top of another. I feel like I'm fighting a war."

"This is exactly like a war—and we're losing."

"Aren't you a bright ray of sunshine."

"Try not to think about it, Aaron. If it weren't for your preparations and smart choices, we'd all be dead."

"Even more refreshing."

Mason patted Aaron on the knee. "Just keep on, keeping

on."

At the last house on a block, above the lapping floodwaters, Aaron ran into a garage and pulled open the door to an upright freezer. It was full of packages of meat, still frozen. He went to the cart and grabbed the orange crate, taking it back to the garage. The meat in the freezer filled the crate. He hauled it to the golf cart, using the bungee cords to tie it down. The cargo area was now full.

He climbed back into the passenger seat and zipped down the curtain. "We've got a full load. Let's go home. We'll drop off this stuff and head back out."

Mason nodded. He rolled into the street and began driving. Aaron had to give him directions to keep him on course through the torrents of rain. The rough ride slowed them down, so they didn't spill any of their cargo.

When they got to the intersection of Aaron's street, Mason slammed on the brakes. A man had crawled into the street and was weakly waving an arm. Aaron recognized him. He didn't know him well, but he was still a neighbor.

Aaron leaped from the golf cart and went to the soaked man. He fell to his knees. "Are you okay, Mark?"

The man grabbed Aaron's arm. "Can't walk. I tore up my knee. It hurts like hell."

"Where's your wife?"

The man's shoulders shook. "Sharon is dead, the roof collapsed and crushed her. Almost crushed me too. I hobbled into a little corner of my front hall that still has a roof over it. I heard the whistle, but I couldn't move fast enough to catch you. I dragged myself into the street, praying you'd come back."

By this time, Mason joined the two. "How can I help?"

Aaron stood up and looked at the cart. "Let's dump the supplies. We'll come back for them after we get Mark back to the house."

Mason started emptying the cargo space. Meanwhile,

Aaron put an arm around the man's shoulders. "You're safe now. We have shelter, food, and a doc to look at your leg." He looked back at Mason. "Help me get him in the front."

The two gently lifted Mark between them and put him in the passenger seat. Aaron flipped the rear seat down. He climbed up and sat down. Mason drove off as easily as he could. Aaron clenched his jaw at Mark's groans with every bump.

Chapter 18
Additional Reconnaissance

As Aaron rode down the street and turned into his driveway, he wondered how any of his house endured the storm when so many others had not. He shrugged his shoulders. He was grateful.

Mason pulled up close to the open golf cart garage door. Aaron hopped off the back and ran inside. He almost ran into his daughter. "We found another injured person. Go get Ben."

Sandy hurried into the house. A moment later, they were back. Mason was unzipping the side curtain when Ben arrived. "This is Mark, a neighbor. He crawled into the street to make sure we saw him. His knee is messed up."

Ben leaned into the cart and spoke to the man. "Do you hurt anywhere else besides your knee?"

"My back. It hurts whenever I move."

Ben motioned to Mason. "Help me get him out of the cart. Then we'll do a fireman's carry into the tent."

Aaron stepped back to give them room. "Once you get him into the tent, we'll go out to get the gas and the rest of our stuff."

Mason nodded as he and Ben lifted Mark from the cart. He cried out in pain when they moved him.

Aaron winced at the suffering. While Mason and Ben maneuvered the man through the kitchen door, Aaron walked outside. He looked down the hill. No question the water was rising. He could only estimate how much. However, now was the time to start measuring it. Aaron went back inside the garage and rummaged around in his cabinets. Shortly, he found what he was looking for—American flags, about two feet tall.

He grabbed a few of them and went outside, walking two houses down the hill to the edge of the lapping water. He stuck the first flag in the ground at the margin of the floodwaters. Then he backed up and stuck flags in the ground, two feet apart, toward his house.

Mason was waiting for him in front of the garage. "Good idea. Those brightly colored flags will help us see how fast the water's rising."

"Yeah, we'll keep track of the water levels from now on. Let's go get the stuff we left behind."

Mason drove the golf cart to the intersection and helped Aaron load up the gas, propane, and bag full of food. When they got back to the house, Mike met them at the garage door. "Let me give you guys a hand with this."

Aaron handed him the bag of food. "Here, give this to Angie."

"She's asleep in the tent."

"Is she? It's good to see the Iron Lady get off her feet."

Sandy came to join the men. "I'll put away the food. I'm glad Mom is getting some rest. I think she needs it more than anybody."

"Thanks, Sweetie. She was awake all night. Hope she sleeps for a while."

"We're about the only people awake. All the new people went back to bed. Even Amy laid down."

"What about Ben?"

"The last I looked he was working on that man you brought in. He's hurtin'. Doc gave him something for the pain."

"What about the woman?"

"Ben's tried to do things for her. He's leaving her alone with her husband. That doesn't sound good. Everything we're doing is falling apart."

Aaron gave Sandy a nudge into the laundry room and pulled the pocket door closed. He took her by the shoulders and stared into her eyes. "Listen. We've got a dozen people out there who are suffering, have lost everything, and are scared to death. About the only thing keeping them from losing it completely, is us. You need to keep your feelings under control. The last thing we need is to let panic creep in. Follow your mother's lead."

Sandy nodded her head. "You're right. I'm sorry."

Aaron went on. "If they aren't sleeping, keep 'em busy. Mason and I will go out again to survey the situation, look for more survivors, and pick up things we can use. While we're gone, you're in charge."

Well, shit, Dad. I thought you were going to give me an easy job."

"There aren't any."

Aaron walked back and pulled the door open. "You need to start thinking about fixing some food for everyone. Get started on that until we get back."

"Okay, Daddy. Mom talked to the command center. You're supposed to call them back."

"Anything new?"

"Not for us."

"I'll take the radio with me so if he calls, I can talk to him."

Mason was waiting for the two when they came out of the laundry room. "While you guys were talking, I opened the front door and pulled back the tent flap to allow fresher air in. If you're finished, we can go. Let's take two golf carts this time."

Aaron blinked his eyes and looked at Mason. "Why?"

"Standard patrol routine. Take two vehicles in case one of them poops out."

Aaron didn't say anything. He nodded and headed for the garage, grabbing the radio, unzipping his coverall, and stuffing it into the holster on his hip. He turned back to Mason. "Go outside and see which of the other golf carts has the most gas? Strip the golf bags off the back, and throw them in the yard."

Mason pulled his coverall hoodie over his head and stepped out into the rain.

While he was gone, Sandy helped Aaron drag the grill back to the open garage door. "Get this thing running again. We need more pasta and hot coffee. Mason and I are going now."

"Be careful out there."

"We'll be back as soon as we can."

Aaron pulled up his hoodie and went out the cart garage door. He unzipped the side curtain and slipped into the seat. Mason steered the extra golf cart next to Aaron's. The two drove off.

Aaron made a small detour to his row of flags. The water had risen halfway up the first flag. He got out of the cart and walked to the edge of the flood. Mason joined him.

"You have more experience with this than me. How much more can the water rise before it gets to the driveway?"

Mason looked up the hill. "Maybe six or seven feet."

"If it continues to rain, we'll be underwater before tomorrow morning."

"Terrific. We need to do something before it gets dark."

"Like what? Build a dam? With what? Even if we had sand and bags, we don't have the manpower to fill them."

"We have a little time, Aaron. Let's both think about it while we're driving around."

"Alright, let's go. I'll take the lead. We need to see how far the water has risen up the rest of the hill."

"At least we don't have such a big area to search."

Aaron climbed back into the golf cart and zipped the curtain. He repeated the winding course from earlier, driving around the wreckage. Mason was close behind. Aaron could hardly see him in the rear-view mirror. The rain continued to fall in waves.

They drove through the intersection where they found Mark lying in the street. At each corner, Aaron worked his way down the side streets as far as he could, stopping to unzip the curtain and blow his whistle. After several blasts, he listened, hoping to hear people yelling over the storm. Each time he retraced his steps to the main street, joining Mason who drove in the other direction.

Directly ahead, the main road dipped down from the crest

of the hill. It disappeared into the water and debris. To the left, a short street ended in a cul-de-sac. Aaron turned his cart onto the street, splashing water as he drove.

At the end, a house stood almost intact. Several golf carts were parked on the driveway. Aaron didn't need to blow his whistle. A man was standing in front of the garage door, wearing a poncho, holding an umbrella and waving his arms. Both Mason and Aaron stopped on the street and got out of their carts.

The man hurried up to them. "I don't know where you guys came from, but I'm glad to see you."

Aaron shook the man's hand. I'm Aaron Colson. This is my son-in-law, Mason."

"I'm Ray Steiner. We were beginning to think everybody evacuated—or were dead."

"How many people do you have?"

"Ten. Four neighbor couples came here when the storm blew their houses to bits. My wife and I have done what we could, which is not much."

Mason edged in, under the umbrella. "Anybody need medical care?"

"Nothing critical. Lots of cuts and bruises."

Aaron wiped water from his face. "Sounds like you were lucky. Tell me your situation."

"We've been without power for two days. We ate out of cans for as long as they lasted. How about you?"

"There are fifteen people at my place. I have a lot less house standing than you, but we still have power because I have a generator. We've been cooking on my grill, so there's hot food."

"We could use some. We haven't eaten anything hot since the day before yesterday. Have you been able to talk to anyone? It's terrible not knowing anything."

"I'm in contact with The Villages command center on a two-way radio."

"Have they sent any help?"

"Nope. They can't get to us. The Villages are flooded with only the tops of the hills still above water. The guy I've been talking to says the rain will continue the rest of today and tonight before the storms begin moving north."

"That ain't good. The water is at my front door. Even with everything closed, the water is still coming in."

"You're about ten feet lower than my place. For the moment we're still mostly dry."

Mason kicked his feet at the water covering the driveway. "You can't stay here."

Aaron completed that thought. "No, you can't. We need to get you to safety. Can we come inside, so I can talk to everyone?"

"Sure-—wade right in."

Mason followed Aaron through the front door and into the living room. The light from a few flickering candles barely penetrated the gloom.

Four men were sitting on one couch with three women on another. A woman, Ray introduced as his wife, was sitting on a reclining chair. All of them had their legs up to keep their feet from getting wet in the two inches of water flowing across the floor.

"Okay everybody," said Ray, "This is Aaron and Mason. They've come to take us away from this mess."

A general cry of relief echoed in the room.

Aaron put on his brightest smile. "Good morning. We're also stranded on the top of the hill. At least part of my house is still dry."

He went on to give an account of the conditions at his house and the people who found shelter there. "We have a doc. If any of you need medical care, he'll fix you up. My generator is giving us power for the refrigerator and the microwave, and I've got a big grill we're using to cook hot food. The first order of business after we get you moved will be something to eat."

Ray settled on a tall stool. "Excuse me. We're grateful for

the help, but you said you have fifteen people in your home. How are you going to manage with ten more?"

Aaron shrugged. "Not easily." He swished his boot through the water. "I don't see how you have any choice. This place is already flooding, and it's getting worse. We have to get you folks out of here."

None of the haggard people in the room disputed this obvious truth.

Mason used the moment to address practical matters. "You may have things here to help us. Do you have any gas or propane?"

"I've got five gallons of gas and a whole bottle of propane."

Aaron was thinking ahead. "Until the last few hours, you've been out of the weather. Do you have any dry clothing, towels, and blankets?"

Ray's wife had the answer. "I've got lots. My name is Maria, by the way. How are you going to keep the clothes from getting wet when we go outside?"

"We brought a bunch of big, plastic trash bags. Go get them, Mason."

"I'll be right back."

Aaron turned back to Ray. "You said you've been eating out of cans. Do you have anything in your freezer?"

"Quite a bit. There wasn't any way to cook it. With the power out so long, I think most of the stuff is spoiled."

"Have you kept the freezer closed?"

"Yeah. No reason to get in there."

"Then it's probably still good. We'll take it along. We're going to need all the food we can get our hands on to feed two dozen people."

Maria motioned to one of the women. " We didn't open the refrigerator either. We'll see if there's anything in there which hasn't gone bad." The two went around the corner to the kitchen.

Mason came back in with the wooden crate and trash bags.

"Let's get started packing up. The water's rising out there. Looks like we got here right on time."

Ray nodded. "That's for sure."

A flurry of activity over the next thirty minutes emptied drawers of shorts, T-shirts and other casual wear. Maria found two dozen eggs in her refrigerator and several bags of cheese. She put them carefully in the bottom of the crate. Mason went to the garage for the gas and disconnected the propane tank from the grill on the patio.

The water on the floor was now ankle deep. Aaron described what was next. "Assuming all your golf carts start, we'll pull them up to the front door one at a time. Each of you go to your cart, and we'll use these umbrellas to keep you and the bags dry while you get in. When everyone has loaded, I'll lead the way. Mason will follow our little wagon train in case anyone has trouble."

One of the golf carts didn't start. Aaron motioned Ray into his cart, while Maria got in with Mason. Aaron flipped the back seat down and transferred the gas, propane, and the apple crate to the cargo space.

When everyone settled in their carts Aaron pulled out of the driveway, zipping the side curtains down to keep out the rain,. The others flowed in behind him. He had glossed over the situation he was creating in his own home and the people there. He glanced back at the apple crate, filled with the food they recovered from the freezer and refrigerator.

Even with the extra food, it would be a challenge to feed two-dozen people. He knew there was only enough for a couple more meals. He hoped Mason and Sandy could put together some stew or chili or something like it.

It'll be standing room only at my house. Gotta keep it together.

He eased onto the street, and the caravan of six golf carts began to wind their way home.

Chapter 19
More Survivors

<u>Noon, Wednesday</u>

Evan Driscoll looked around the studio at the Weather Channel. It was a mess.

Too many people, too much going on.

John Meyers came over to Evan's chair. "Have you seen the latest storm track?"

"Not much to see. Those hurricanes haven't moved for two days."

"Central Florida is getting hammered. Any idea how much rain they've had?"

"Estimates. Information from the area is hard to come by. What little news we're getting says they're measuring rainfall in feet. There are thousands of national guard, FEMA personnel, and first responders standing by on the margins of the storms. With all the roads flooded, no surface traffic is moving. They're flying in helicopters, and using boats."

Meyers read off a sheet of paper. "Both coasts have suffered catastrophic damage, everything from the Space Coast to Tampa. In between, the Orlando metropolitan area was shredded by Karl and flooded. Casualties are in the thousands."

"We haven't heard from Aaron for two days. I worry about him."

"His big retirement community is right in the bullseye."

A staffer came over and handed Evan the latest forecast. "Here's some news. The big dome of high pressure covering the southeast is drifting north. That's good for Florida. The hurricanes will start moving, and by tomorrow morning, they could start drying out."

"Good for Florida. What about us in Atlanta?"

"These are the most extreme weather conditions in history. A lot of what's happening to Florida could hit us."

❖

Angie stood by the open garage door, wiping the sleep from her eyes as she looked out into the rain.

Sandy walked over and stood next to her. "I wanted you to sleep longer."

"I slept enough." Angie puffed her cheeks. "I've stopped telling myself this was the worst storm I've ever seen."

"The worst storm any of us have ever seen. Dad and Mason have been gone for a while. I hope they're okay."

The two turned away from the open garage door and headed back to the kitchen.

"I can't think of anybody to count on more than your father."

"That's for sure. Dad keeps us moving in the right direction."

"It's easier for him with Mason as a right-hand."

"They're a good team. We're lucky. I still worry about them."

"How long have they been gone?"

"A couple hours."

"Is everyone still asleep?"

"You're the only person not sleeping since the guys left. Are you sure you don't need more?"

"Of course, I do."

"I could use a little more sleep myself." Amy yawned as she came around the corner from the tent.

Angie gathered her in a warm hug. "How's your patient doing?"

"We now have two. Aaron and Mason found another survivor.

"They did? Who?"

"A guy name Mark."

"Mark Reynolds? His wife's name is Sharon. I play Mahjong with her. Did she come with him?"

"They brought him alone. His knee is torn up and his back's killing him Ben put a brace on his knee. He also has an injury to his back. Not much Ben can do about that. He gave him something for the pain."

"I hope he's not the neighbor we know. What about Cheri?"

Amy's whole body drooped. "I've stopped asking about her. She's slipping away from us. About all I can do is keep her warm and dry. Ben shakes his head whenever he takes her blood pressure. These people need to be evacuated. Don't suppose there's much chance of that."

"I talked to the command center before I went to sleep. Nobody's coming today. Go get your cup and I'll pour you some coffee. We both need a pick-me-up."

Amy ducked back into the tent. Angie turned to the coffee pot. "Damn. There's no power. The generator must have run out of gas."

Sandy patted her mother's shoulder as she headed for the garage. "I can do this. I'll get us up and running in no time."

"Thanks, honey."

Angie put her hands on the coffee pot as Amy came back with her cup. "The generator ran out of gas again. Sandy went to fill it up. I think this coffee is still hot enough."

"Hot or cold, it doesn't matter. Did Aaron and Mason go out again?"

"Yeah, they went looking for more survivors."

"What are we going to do if they find more people?"

Angie leaned against a kitchen counter and shook her head. "If they do, they'd better bring along some food, cause what we have left is not going to last."

"I've been so busy helping Ben. I haven't paid much attention to anything—or anybody else. Are things worse?"

Angie was about to say something when the coffee pot light came back on. "The generator is running again." She went to the refrigerator and took out the creamer. "Here's a little something for your coffee."

"I feel like I should be doing more to help."

"You are helping, Amy. It's a big load off Aaron, knowing you and Ben are doing all you can taking care of our injured."

"The drive from Punta Gorda was a nightmare. Since then, it's been one awful thing after another. I feel bad how I've acted."

"No time for regrets now. I doubt Aaron and Mason are giving it any thought. What they can see is how you've focused on making a difference in the place where neither one of them can do much, taking care of hurt people."

"Mason talked to me yesterday. It helped a lot. He probably still thinks I'm a wimp."

"No, he doesn't. I'll bet he's seen much worse. You aren't a warrior, and he knows it."

"I should tell him I'm sorry."

"You don't have to do that either."

Sandy walked into the kitchen while the two were talking. "Whatever you think you need to say, say it. While I was filling the generator tank, I saw the lights of golf carts working their way down the street. Looks like we have more company."

Rain splashed off the windshield of the cart. Aaron peered into the gloom, weaving around a minefield of obstacles. A glance in his rear mirror showed Mason and the rest of the carts behind.

Ray Steiner was riding with him. "How you can see where you're going?"

"The only reason I can is because I've been this way a couple of times."

"None of us have been out of the house much in the past two days. I hope they don't freak out with all this destruction. Even worse, I've seen bodies mixed in with it. I was a fireman for thirty years, so it's not like I've never seen corpses."

"Man, am I glad you have that background. You can bet this is terrifying to your friends. You have to help me keep 'em settled down."

"Mason acts like this is nothing new to him. He's a good man."

"Mason served three tours in Afghanistan. In any case, I couldn't have managed without his help. We both need you. Mason was injured driving up here from Punta Gorda. He's been doing what he has, because he had too. Maybe he'll take a breath and get some rest when he finds out there's some real help."

"I'll do whatever I can."

"Good, because we're almost home. With your bunch, we'll hardly have room to move around."

Aaron drove through the intersection where they found Mark and turned up his street. He pointed ahead. "See the lantern on the lamp post? That's my place."

"It's torn to pieces. How have you managed?"

"I couldn't begin to tell you. You'll have to see for yourself."

As he looked in his mirror, the other golf carts followed closely as Aaron weaved his way around rooftops, furniture, bushes, and trees strewn along his route. He turned into his driveway and to the open garage where he angled his cart parallel with the door. The other carts parked on the driveway, filling it up. Mason came last, squeezing in among the carts.

Aaron quickly unzipped his curtain and stepped out of his cart. Mason was as fast. They opened umbrellas and shepherded the new arrivals out of their carts and into the garage.

Angie greeted them as they came in, introducing herself in warmth and serenity. Sandy bustled around the garage, setting up folding chairs and apologizing there weren't enough for everyone. Amy moved from person to person, asking if they had any injuries.

Aaron stood aside. He smiled at the cool efficiency of his ladies. He looked over at Mason, who raised his eyebrows and cocked his head with a little nod.

The hubbub stirred the four men slumbering in the

makeshift sleeping area in the corner. Soon there were more greetings, more introductions, and smatterings of shared experiences over the past two days.

Aaron used the sociability of the moment, signaling Mason to slip back outside and bring in the gas, bags of dry clothes, and the orange crate of food. They piled everything on the folding tables.

Angie excused herself from a woman and came to stand next to Aaron. "What's all this stuff?"

"Things we need. I got another can of gas, extra propane, and," pointing to the orange crate, "more food. Something else, everyone will appreciate—dry clothes, towels, and blankets."

"How'd that happen?"

"The house these people came from, didn't get knocked down in the hurricane, so there was a lot of dry clothing. We bundled them up in the trash bags and brought them back."

"If they had a whole house, how come they left?"

"We arrived as the house was flooding, so they had to leave. They also had no way to prepare meals. We emptied the freezer and brought home food we can cook."

Angie stepped closer to Aaron and half-whispered. "Even with this extra food, and what we have left, I don't think it will last very long."

"Do the best you can."

Angie opened the trash bag and started setting the food on the table, "We can fry up this hamburger. I'll get Sandy and Mason to make us a kettle of chili."

"You do that, sweetie. These new people are plenty hungry, and the rest will want to eat too."

Ray Steiner walked over to Aaron and Angie. "Did I hear you were going to make some chili? I can help. All those years in the firehouse made me a decent cook."

"Mason can use a hand. He and my daughter, Sandy, own a restaurant in Punta Gorda."

"Great. We'll cook up a pot of hot chili."

Aaron pulled Ray a little closer. "We may have gotten you out of your house before it flooded, but the situation is still pretty grim here. Let me show you something and get all your people together, and I'll tell them what we're facing."

Ray followed Aaron to the garage doorway. He pointed down the street to his row of flags. "I put those flags out a couple of hours ago. Look at the first flag."

"I can only see the top of it."

"It was uncovered when I put it in. That means the water has risen over a foot and will reach the driveway in about twelve hours. The Villages planners built all the houses above the streets, which will give us another couple of hours before the water starts running into my house like it did yours."

Ray glanced at his watch. "Fourteen hours. We'll be flooded out before dawn tomorrow."

"That's what I'm afraid of. Only this time, none of us have anywhere to go. We need to come up with something before the sun goes down six hours from now."

"What do you have in mind?"

"Fragments and half-baked ideas. I haven't had much time to run it through my brain with all we've been doing."

You'd better have something planned before you talk to everyone."

Mason came out of the kitchen with a cast-iron skillet. He listened to Aaron and Ray as he turned on the grill and dumped hamburger into the skillet. "I saw the flag too."

Aaron turned away from the open door. "Got any great ideas?"

"No more than you. Let me cook some food and feed everybody."

Ray walked around the grill to stand next to Mason. "I can give you a hand with this. You look like you could use a rest."

Aaron joined them. "Yeah, Mason, you're limping worse

than ever. You need to get off your feet."

"Right about that. I've had it."

"Let Ben take a look at your wound."

Mason looked around. "Speaking of which, where is Ben? Amy went in to get him, so he could look at these new people."

At that moment, Amy and Ben came out the kitchen door. He spoke softly to the newest survivors on his way over to the grill. Aaron could tell from the look on his face, he didn't have good news.

Ben came around the grill and pushed Mason and Aaron into the corner, next to the open garage door. He barely murmured to them. "Cheri died. Simon is still asleep. I didn't want to wake him until I talked to you."

Aaron pursed his lips and shook his head. "Shit. This couldn't have happened at a worse time."

Mason put a hand on Ben's shoulder. "I'm sorry, Doc. I know you did all you could."

"Which was not much. I feel like a second-class witch doctor."

Mason turned back to Aaron. "We need to move the body from the tent."

"Not you. Ben, I want you to look at Mason's injuries. Fix him up the best you can. Give him something for the pain and knock him out. He needs to rest."

Mason waved his hands in dismissal like he was declining a penalty. "No sedatives, Aaron. Too much happening. I'll get some sleep."

Ray continued stirring the cooking meat. "I heard most of that. What can I do to help?"

Aaron smiled at the newcomer. "You're doing it. I'll get my wife and daughter to pitch in." He gestured to Mike, standing at the edge of the crowd, to join him. "Meanwhile, we'll take Cheri out the front door. I don't want to bring her through here."

"Do it quietly," cautioned Ben. "Don't wake those sleeping

women in the tent, or Simon."

"Mike and I will go first and carry the body outside. You and Mason come behind and settle in your medical corner so you can change his bandages and whatever else you need to do."

Aaron turned to Mike, who walked over while he was talking. "You and I have to do this with the least amount of disturbance possible. All our people know there are fatalities out there. Having a corpse lying ten feet from where they're sleeping is an entirely different thing."

Mike took a deep breath, rubbing his hand across his face. He grabbed a coverall. "Lead the way."

Chapter 20
Overloaded

<u>Mid-Day Wednesday</u>

The tent was dark. Aaron led Mike to Ben's medical corner behind a room divider. Soundlessly, the two men picked up Cheri's body and carried her out the front door.

When they got outside, Aaron guided them around the corner of the house to get her out of sight. The last thing he wanted was a dead body lying in his front yard where anyone could see it.

The two put Cheri down gently. Aaron picked up some palm fronds and covered the body. "That's all we can do for her. Let's get inside, away from this infernal rain."

As they headed back to the open garage door, the radio on Aaron's hip came to life. "Command center to Aaron. Come in, Aaron."

"Get in out of the rain, Mike. I need to give the command center a report."

Aaron unzipped the side curtain on his golf cart, parked next to the garage. He slipped into the seat and zipped the curtain closed.

Ben had stood aside as Aaron and Mike carried Cheri's body away. Now, he motioned Mason to drop his shorts and lay down. Mason's bandages were soaked with blood. The medic pulled away the bandages and looked at Mason's wounds. He leaned over and muttered, "You've managed to pull some of your staples loose. Plus, some more shrapnel has worked its way out. I'm going to give you a shot for pain before I start."

"Whatever you say, Doc."

Ben tapped a dispenser of local anesthesia around and across the wounds before he began. He worked quietly for several minutes, extracting small pieces of metal and re-stapling Mason's torn flesh.

When he finished, Ben put on new bandages. He leaned down and whispered again. "Some of the places you didn't tear are starting to heal. Your butt is a bloody mess, but if you can manage to take it easy, it will get better."

"I already feel better."

"Because I gave you a healthy dose of pain medication. Why don't you do as Aaron said and get some rest."

Mason pulled a pillow under his head. "Don't let me sleep more than a couple hours."

Ben watched as Mason relaxed. His eyes closed, and he could swear he was already asleep.

Aaron keyed the button on his radio. "Aaron to command center."

"This is Scott. Been awhile. What's your situation?"

"We've been out twice this morning. The first time was to look around and find some supplies. We found another injured man. The second time was to sweep the top of the hill and look for more survivors. We brought back ten people."

"How many people are you sheltering?"

"Twenty-five—no, make that twenty-four. The lady our Doc was taking care of died."

"I'm sorry. What about the other injury?"

"A man hurt his knee and back when his house fell on him and killed his wife. Can you get a helicopter in here and start evacuating us?"

"There aren't any helicopters here right now. They took a load of our most serious injuries out after they dropped off supplies."

"I suppose still no boats."

"Negative. There's still too much junk in the water for our light boats to make their way. FEMA and the National Guard are moving pontoon boats in, but it will be awhile before they can get here."

Aaron clenched his fists in frustration. "Look, Scott, things are pretty tough here. I have more people than we can handle. We're running out of food and hope. Even worse, the water's still rising. By dawn tomorrow morning it will flood the remains of my house. Then our situation will turn from terrible to critical. We already have one dead. I don't know how many other survivor groups you're talking to, but you have to do something for the two-dozen people we have here."

There was a pause, and then Scott came back. "You've got a bigger group than the other neighborhood survival shelters I'm talking too. I haven't been able to contact some of them at all. You can be sure my first-priority will be to get you out of there. I don't know when that will be."

There was a sharp edge to Aaron's voice. "What do you expect me to tell these desperate people?"

"Tell them there are thousands, tens of thousands, of people waiting for the earliest possible second to start providing real aid. Everybody in the country knows what a fix you're in. Rescue crews are as desperate to get in as you are to get out."

Aaron took a deep breath. "Sorry if I sounded panicky. What about the weather forecast?"

"The hurricanes are starting to move north. We expect the rain to continue the rest of today, but slacking off by tomorrow morning."

"Not much help for us right now. Any idea how much rain we've had?"

"Best guess from when this started is about four feet."

Aaron whistled into the radio. "No wonder we're flooding. That's got to be a record."

"No doubt. Do you still have power?"

"Yeah. We found enough gas to keep the generator running today and through the night, and enough propane for the grill. We're still cooking hot meals for now, but after we feed everyone today, the cupboard will be bare. Even worse, the water will flood this house before dawn tomorrow."

Aaron waited for a response. It seemed like a long time before Scott came back. "Everyone around here is frankly astonished at what you've done. You've given people shelter, food, and medical aid without any help at all. You even went out and found more survivors. We have a big rescue operation ready to go as soon as we can. Your group is at the top of the list when we do."

"Thanks for that. I'll tell my people. It'll lift their spirits."

"If anything changes, let me know."

"You're at the top of my list."

"Roger, out."

Scott pushed the microphone across the desk and sat back.

From behind him, a voice spoke. "Don't make promises you can't keep."

Scott spun his chair around and faced the man in charge of the command center. "I didn't say any more than what we're planning to do."

"We have our hands full taking care of the survivors already packed into this shelter. The isolated group you've been talking to, will have to wait."

"Maybe, but this group is different. They now have twenty-four people stuffed into an improvised shelter. They even did a rescue operation of their own. They have power, water, food, and a doctor to care for the injured."

"So, they're stable. Even more reason to let us concentrate on the crisis we have here, now."

"They won't be stable tomorrow morning when they get flooded out."

"You don't know that. Stay in contact. If their situation gets critical, we'll try to help."

Aaron unzipped his coverall and put the radio back in the holster on his belt.

Who does he think he's kidding? Scott tried to make me feel better, but no one's coming. We're on our own.

He stepped out of the golf cart. The relentless rain made him feel fifty pounds heavier. He walked a few feet down the driveway. The clutter of golf carts made him step around them to get a look at his flags. The water covered half his second flag. He shook his head and headed back to the open garage door. He stopped half-way and looked back at the golf carts. Then he looked around at the ruins of the nearby homes.

Maybe we can build a dam.

As he stepped inside, Ray and Sandy looked up at him from behind the grill. Ray was stirring food in a tall steel pot. Several people were watching him.

He waved at Aaron with a wooden spoon. "We've made up the most original mixture you ever saw. It might not be the most authentic chili I ever made, but there's a lot of it."

"When will it be ready?"

"Angie's heating another bowl of pasta in the microwave. When she's finished, we'll dump it in here, mix it up, and be set to go."

"No more waiting. I've got the pasta right here." Angie came from the kitchen, a steaming bowl in her hands.

Ray clapped his hands. "Great. Wonderful. Pour it right in." He turned back to Aaron. "I'm going to call this chilighetti."

A bubble of laughter filled the air. Aaron laughed too. "Serve it up. Save a little for me."

Sandy sounded off. "Soups on. Everybody, line up and get a plate and utensils."

Aaron made conversation with each person as they got a plate of food.

Soon, all the chairs were full, and people were sitting with their backs to the garage walls, some of them enjoying their first hot meal in two days. It looked to Aaron as if about everyone was there. He got Sandy's attention. "Is Mason sleeping?"

"Out like a light. He needs sleep more than food."

"Set something aside for him to eat later."

Aaron saw Ben coming out of the kitchen. He stopped when Aaron signaled him, and the two retreated to the laundry room. "Sandy says Mason is asleep. Where's Simon?"

"He's still asleep too. He didn't wake up when we carried his wife outside. I looked at him now when I was checking on Mark. He must be exhausted. I didn't wake him to eat."

"What about everybody else?"

"I did initial first-aid on the new people you brought back. Some of them have serious cuts. I need to do more work. All of them are tired and worn down."

"I know. It's going to get worse before it gets better."

"I hope you've got a good pep talk ready."

Eventually, Aaron got his plate filled. He sat down against the garage door. The mixture of chili and pasta was satisfying, and it filled him up. Mike came by and poured him a glass of water from a plastic bottle.

When he finished, Aaron got up and added his paper plate and plastic utensils to a trash can. Then he ambled over to his wife. "Looks like your meal was a success."

"We can do this one more time, maybe. Feeding this many people use up our supplies pretty fast."

"Even with the stuff we brought back?"

"It helped, but we're still running out."

"One more thing to add to the 'what are we going to do about that' list?"

"Tell me I'm wrong, but I have the feeling food is not the main thing on your mind."

Aaron stepped close to his wife and almost whispered. "You aren't wrong. Still as perceptive as ever, Sweetie."

Angie looked in her husband's eyes and murmured back. "What is the main thing?"

"It's the rising water. We have to do something about it

today, or we'll be swimming by morning."

"Got a plan? You must have a plan."

Aaron winked at her. "Finish your lunch."

Most of the people were setting back in chairs or against the walls. They were chatting with each other. Aaron was glad the mood was so light. It would make it easier to deliver a more solemn speech.

He walked to the open space in the middle of the garage and raised his hand for attention. The group went silent at once. "There's nothing like a hot, filling meal to raise your spirits. Kudos to our cooks." Aaron raised his arm to point at Ray, Sandy, and Angie. A cheer echoed through the garage, along with applause.

"We should also thank Ray and his wife Maria for these dry clothes. You won't win any fashion awards, but I think you look great."

There was laughter as people pointed at each other's mismatched, ill-fitting clothing.

"A little while ago, I talked again to the command center, which is coordinating the care of the many people who have found shelter there. Tell you the truth, I don't think their conditions are much better than ours. The difference, of course, is we're stranded on top of this hill which used to be our neighborhood. The floodwaters have made islands of The Villages."

Aaron paused. No one was laughing now. Every eye looked straight at him.

"My guy in the command center says the hurricanes have started moving north. They expect the rain to stop by tomorrow morning. That means rescue crews can finally reach us by either boat or helicopter. The end of this misery is in sight."

A wave of relief washed over the faces of everyone.

Aaron seized the moment to deliver the bad news. "However, the rain is still falling. Our island is getting smaller by the minute. Unless we buy ourselves some time, the water will continue to rise and will flood this house before dawn tomorrow. Those of you who came from Ray's house know what I'm talking about."

Ray added his own exclamation point. "It was horrible. I never felt so helpless."

Aaron went on. "What we are going to do is build sort of a dam. We can't wait and go stumbling around in the dark tonight, so we'll work today and hope it's enough.

"We'll work in shifts, partly to spread out the work between us, and partly because I only have six sets of coveralls for the people working outside."

Sandy asked the question on every mind. "How you gonna build this dam?"

"I got the idea when I was outside last. We can ... "

"Where the hell is my wife?" came a bellow from the kitchen door.

Aaron turned. A red-faced Simon glowered at him.

Ben ran over to Simon. "Take it easy. Let's go back inside, so we can talk."

Simon screamed. "I don't want to talk. I want to know where my wife is."

Aaron frowned and looked at the shock on people's faces. He couldn't let this outburst continue. "Excuse me for a moment."

Ben was still trying to push Simon back into the house and getting nowhere. Aaron rushed over, and between the two of them shoved Simon into the laundry room. Aaron slid the pocket door closed. Ben grabbed Simon by the shoulders and looked straight into his eyes. "Your wife is dead. She died while you were sleeping. I'm very sorry."

"Where is she?"

"Mike and Aaron carried her out the front door."

Simon screamed again. "What did you do—haul her outside and dump her with the rest of the trash?"

Ben was all business. "We took her outside to protect the

living."

Simon's face was full of rage. "You. You're supposed to be a doctor. You just let her die."

"I did all I could."

"Nobody did anything. You let her die."

A flash of anger boiled up inside Aaron. He pushed past Ben, grabbed Simon by the front of his shirt, and shoved him against the wall. "Look, we're sorry about Cheri, but I have two-dozen people to keep alive. We're in a hell of a mess here, and you aren't helping a bit. Shut up and stay out of the way."

Tears filled Simon's eyes. He lowered his head and sobbed. His shoulders shook.

Ben was consoling. "I feel terrible about this, but Aaron's right. There's a bigger danger to everyone. The time to grieve is not now.

Aaron forced himself to be calm. "What about you, Simon? You must be hungry. There's food in the garage. Why don't we join the others?"

Still sobbing, Simon meekly let Aaron and Ben lead him out of the laundry room and into the garage.

Aaron would forever be grateful to Ray for jumping up and running over to Simon. "What a tragedy. We're all sorry for you."

Everyone in the garage got to their feet and joined Ray, speaking words of comfort and sympathy to the crying man.

Chapter 21
Damn, Dam

Aaron stood aside as the survivors drew a wretched Simon to them, offering him condolences and support. Sandy went to the chili pot and spooned up a plateful of food. She took it and a glass of water to Simon. A woman jumped up from her chair and invited him to sit and eat.

The drumming of the rain on the garage roof made a background of steady racket like standing next to a freeway at rush hour. Added to that were the murmurs of twenty people talking to each other and in small groups. It always amazed him that people could have private conversations in a crowd.

Aaron signaled Mike and Ray to join him in the corner behind the grill. "Before Simon came out, I was about to tell everyone my idea for building a dam against the rising water. While they're all busy, maybe I should tell you guys my plan. You might be able to think of better ways to do it."

Ray idly stirred the last of the chili. "What's your idea?"

"Let me tell you what I know. First, the command center says they expect the rain to stop by tomorrow morning. Next, this house is at the top of the hill, which means we will flood last. Mason and I put flags out this morning to see how fast the water was rising. My guess is we will have about fourteen hours before the water gets to us, which would be sometime during the night."

Ray waved his spoon at Aaron. "I get it. We put a barrier up across the driveway to hold back the water. It wouldn't need to be very big, or last very long. If it stops raining and the water begins to recede, we might not get wet."

Aaron nodded his head. "That's right."

Mike had a question of his own. "How are we going to build a dam?"

"We take the golf carts, and lay them on their sides in a line from the front door to right here." Aaron pointed to the open corner of the garage.

"That becomes our base, an anchor, to hold back the water. We can cut up some tarps and wrap them around the carts to seal the openings around the wheels. Then we go out in the rubble and bring back doors, sheets of plywood, anything flat and sturdy, to put against the carts like a wall to hold back the water. We can pile more trash against the barrier to hold our doors and wood upright. It will still leak, but I think our miniature dam might hold until the water starts to go down."

Both men looked out the garage door. Ray came to a conclusion first. "We might get away with it."

Mike wasn't so sure. "You think golf carts and bedroom doors will hold back all that water?"

Aaron shrugged and nodded. "That's the plan."

"It's crazy."

"You have a better idea? Now's the time."

"No, I don't. Maybe Ray's right, it might work."

"It better work, 'cause I'm out of options."

Aaron looked over at the crowd, still talking eagerly with each other. He turned back to the two, stepped closer and murmured "One thing is for sure. None of these people can know we have any doubts. As far as they're concerned, we have a plan to keep the water from flooding them out."

Ray and Mike flanked Aaron as he took out his whistle and blew it. People stopped talking and turned to him.

"Okay everybody, let me finish telling you our situation. As I was saying, we can expect no help from outside until tomorrow, at the earliest. Meanwhile, the rain continues to fall and the water is rising. It will flood us out by dawn tomorrow, so we must work together and do something today.

"We're gonna build a makeshift dam across the front of the house and driveway using the golf carts laid over on their sides and things like doors, anything we can find, as a wall against the water.

"We'll start with a crew of six, partly because that's how many pairs of waterproof coveralls I have, and partly to switch off and share the load as the work wears us out. Ray, Mike and I will be in the first shift. I need three more volunteers."

Aaron grinned as hands went up. "That's the spirit. We'll get this done in no time. You three guys put on some coveralls."

While they did, Aaron walked over to Ray and Mike. "Get 'em started out there. Before you lay the golf carts over, siphon out the gas. Leave my cart alone. We still need a way to get around. I'll be right out."

Ray motioned to the men who had put on coveralls and led them out.

Aaron excused himself as he weaved around people to the other side of the garage. He pulled out his two biggest tarps from a cubicle. Speaking to no one in particular, he pointed at the tarps. "We need to cut these in two, the long way, to wrap around the golf carts."

Simon Frazier elbowed his way forward. "Let me do it."

Aaron made a steady gaze. "You feel up to it?"

"I gotta do something to keep my mind occupied."

"Okay, let me get a pair of scissors from my tool box."

Aaron started to shoulder his way through the crowd, then stopped and shouted. "About half of you go in the kitchen or the tent. We need more room to work. I'll call you when I need you to relieve the guys working outside."

When the garage got less crowded, Aaron went to his toolbox and handed Simon a pair of scissors. "Think you can cut a straight line?"

Simon took them and nodded. Sandy went to help, and they spread out a tarp, folding it in half. Simon dropped to his knees and began cutting. Aaron walked over to talk with Angie.

❖

Mason could sleep through almost anything, especially when he was so worn out. The chorus of women moving around the tent and talking stirred him. He turned over and leaned against a forearm. His hip and butt throbbed, but the sharp pains he experienced before he went to sleep were gone.

Shot must still be working.

He sat up and shook his head to clear his mind. What were the women talking about? In the overlapping conversations, Mason heard the gist of what they were saying. Something about building a dam against the rising water. He and Aaron talked about it earlier, but his father-in-law rejected the idea because there didn't seem to be any way to do it. Aaron must have figured something out.

In any case, it was time to catch up, no matter how much he wanted to sleep.

When he got to the garage, Sandy was on her knees helping Simon cut a tarp. Aaron was talking to Angie. Mason walked over to them.

Aaron's shoulders sagged when he saw him. "What are you doing awake so soon?"

"It was hard to sleep with so many people coming and going. Are you really trying to build some kind of dam?"

"We're tipping the golf carts over around the garage and the front of the house. Then we'll take the tarps Sandy and Simon are cutting in half to wrap around the bottoms and wheels of the carts facing the water. We'll scrounge up some doors, flat sheets of wood, anything, to lay along the cart wheels."

"How long do you think that's gonna work?"

Aaron shrugged. "Not very long. I hope it lasts through the night. If it quits raining in the morning, we might have bought ourselves enough time."

Mason looked away and ran the plan through his mind. Maybe Aaron was right. So far, his good planning and sound management through this ordeal had kept them a step ahead of the fury of the storms. Anyway, he didn't have a better idea, and it was keeping people busy.

He looked back at Aaron. "What can I do?"

"Feed everyone when they finish working. They'll be hungry. If everything falls apart, it might be the last food they have for a while."

"Don't you need me to work outside?"

"In the first place, gimpy, you're not up to it. In the second place, you can't work outside because someone is wearing your coveralls. And in the last place, where else am I gonna find a cook?"

Angie added something else. "This next meal might be the last because we'll be out of food, at least the kind we can cook on the grill and in the microwave. After that, we'll be eating out of cans."

Aaron rolled his eyes. "I hope someone comes to rescue us before that."

Ray stepped inside the garage door and interrupted them. "Aaron, can you come out here. There's something you need to see."

Aaron pulled his hoodie over his head. "I'll be back. You guys get the grub going."

The rain pelted Aaron as he followed Ray out the door. The men had maneuvered three of the golf carts and tipped them over. Aaron looked sadly at the destruction to the garden he'd spent so much time planting and nurturing.

Ray walked down the driveway, skirting the overturned golf carts. He pointed down the street. "How many flags did you stick in the ground?"

Aaron's heart sank as he looked. Three of the five flags he'd planted were under water. The water was lapping at the farthest flag. "The water's risen six feet, a lot quicker than we thought."

"Yeah, and it'll rise faster, the closer it gets to the top of this hill."

"I think we've only got a couple of hours to finish our dam. We need more people working out here."

"That's what I was going to suggest."

Aaron squared around to stare directly into Ray's eyes. "You and I know what that means. Now we have to go in there and tell our people what it means. We spent a lot of time and effort settling everyone down. We fed them and told them we were building a dam to protect us from these flood waters. Now we gotta mobilize every soul to finish this dam anyway we can. They're gonna know something is seriously wrong."

Ray looked again at the last flags. "When we send them out in this never-ending rain, they're gonna get wet and tired. And all the time, they'll see the water rising. They're gonna lose it."

"My family's not gonna lose it."

"Maybe not. They're a solid bunch. What about the others?"

Aaron shrugged. "I don't know what else to tell them except the simple, plain, unvarnished, garden variety truth."

"I sure wouldn't tell them anything else."

"What about your people?"

Ray glanced at a couple men turning over another golf cart. "Most of my people will be okay. Three of them are out here now. That guy, Mike, was an engineer. He's laying the carts in an arc in front of the garage—says it'll hold the water back better."

"For as long as it lasts. Right now, we need to go back inside, get everyone together, and tell them what we have on our hands."

Mason looked up from the grill when Aaron and Ray came back inside. "I'm cooking another pot of chili to feed everyone when...." He stopped as he saw the grim look on Aaron's face, "What?"

Aaron didn't say anything. He turned to the people lounging around the garage, clapped his hands, and spoke in a loud voice. "Ray and I were outside. The water is coming up the hill faster than we expected. We need to finish building our dam sooner than I thought. My first idea, to send you out six at a time wearing coveralls, is not going to be enough. We'll all have to work outside—starting right now. I know you're going to be wet and miserable, and we can't help that. Ray, Mike, and I will tell you what to do and get you back in here as soon as possible."

Ray added immediacy. "The water will get to our wall in no more than two or three hours. The better job we do, the longer we'll stay dry."

Aaron pointed at one of the women. "Go wake up the people sleeping in the tent. Tell 'em what's going on."

He paused a moment, looking at faces staring back at him with a mixture of fear, reluctance, and indecision. He added the motivation. "So far, we've been lucky, but now this new threat means every one of us have to get busy. Our dam won't hold back the water for long. After that, we'll be flooded out. If that happens during the night, the only safe place left for us will be on the roof."

Everyone glanced up.

"Yeah, the roof. We've come to that."

One of the women asked the obvious question. "How are we going to get up there?"

"I have a ladder. We'll help each other."

A man stepped out of the crowd. "Is that after we wipe ourselves out building your dam? Who do you think we are—a bunch of college kids? I'm already stiff and sore and worn out from doing what we've done, now you expect retired, geriatric people to work like stevedores."

Aaron walked over and stared at the man. "You act like I'm a drill instructor dispensing corporal punishment. I'm as scared as you. I'm fighting for my life—and yours as well. I'm as old as you, and every bit as beat up. I'm doing this because there's no other choice. Now, how about helping us out?"

The man blinked at the stinging rebuke. He looked around at the other anxious faces. "I guess you're right. Sorry about the outburst."

"Forget it. Under the circumstances, I might have done the

same."

As he was talking, Mason and Ray came over to stand next to him. Aaron addressed the whole group. "This is an example of how quickly things can get out of hand. It's not surprising. Our circumstances are crappy and anyone could snap. "Tonight, is going to be even more stressful than today. We've all gotta focus on working together."

Mike stomped in from outside. He grabbed a towel and wiped his face. "It's getting worse. Anybody going to help us?"

Aaron took advantage of the moment. "We all are. Take a minute and tell us how you're organizing the work."

Mike turned to the group and explained what he needed.

When he finished, Aaron spoke softly. "You might be better taking off most of your clothes so you'll have something dry to put on when you come back in. In any case, it's time to get started."

Chapter 22
Soaked and Miserable

Aaron watched people step out of the garage, muttering as the rain dripped from their noses. Men had stripped to their shoes and shorts. Women were nearly as scantily clad. The water clinging to their lips spurted as they grunted and strained. Aaron considered the scene.

If anybody recorded this for Facebook, it would probably go viral—and everyone would think it was a joke.

Mike came out last, carrying the cut tarps, and pointed at the driveway. "We shoved the carts together and lashed them tight. They're in a short arc with the widest part at the top. This way, the water won't have a flat surface to push against."

Aaron nodded. "What's next?"

"We wrap these tarps around the carts, securing them under the wheels. We'll get a couple girls to hold the tarps until we lay anything solid, we can find up against them."

"Looks like the guys have found some of those things in the wreckage."

"It's a good start. Now we have help, we can haul enough to finish the job."

"I'll get out of your way so you can."

Aaron detoured around the overturned carts and walked to his flags. The fourth flag was nearly submerged. Ray joined him and the two stood glumly as the water lapped in ripples around the last flag. The flood now covered the down slope street and half of Aaron's yard.

Aaron used his hand to shield his face from the slanting rain. "I think the water's rising faster."

"I said it would, the closer it got to the top of the hill."

"We can't catch a break. How long before the water gets to our dam?"

"Not long. Two or three hours—if we're lucky."

Aaron turned back to the carts. Several men were straining to lift the wheels off the ground, while women stuffed the edges of the tarps underneath and then held them while others brought demolished home doors to cram against the wheel wells.

Ray leaned into the wind. "We need to finish the wall to resist the water. I'll get our people busy hauling rubbish to pile against the doors. That should keep them upright."

"I hope we have enough time."

Ray yanked his water logged shorts up as he looked over his shoulder. "Me too."

Mason fretted as he paced back and forth behind the grill. With every lap he leaned out the garage door watching the haggard men and women working. He nodded his head in respect. Despite their ages and limited physical resources, they were certainly giving it their all.

Sandy wandered over to her husband. "What's wrong with you?"

"I'm not helping." He pointed outside. "Look at them. Almost panic-stricken people in desperate conditions trying to build a wall against this deluge."

Sandy looked out the garage door. "They're doing the job. Looks like the dam's almost finished. How much help do you think you'd really be?"

"I'm not crippled."

"Yes, you are. You've been running on guts for two days. Save your strength and do what Dad said. Cook some food."

Angie came out the kitchen door. She had an armful of packages of meat. "This about cleans out the freezer. A good thing. Most of this meat is thawed out."

She plopped a roast down on the table. "I also found half a dozen packages of hot dogs."

Mason rolled his eyes. "Who freezes hot dogs?"

"I was saving them for a hurricane."

Mason laughed. "Get me a chopping board and a sharp knife. I'll cut up this roast. How much pasta do we have left?"

"One more meal."

Sandy picked up the kettle. "I'll heat up some water." She hugged Mason. "Feeling useful again?"

"Yeah. Just don't pat me on the butt."

An hour later, Aaron rubbed his hands together letting the rain wash away some of the grime from carrying loads to the dam. His back was sore and his legs felt like they would give out any minute. The gash on his head was raw. The pain never went away.

My kingdom for a chair.

He pushed his misery aside and walked to the middle of the street in front of the house to survey the progress

Mike and Ray divided everyone into two teams. Mike directed the work to finish the dam. His team found more doors and a sheet of plywood mixed in the debris to lay along the row of golf carts. The dam looked finished. Ray's workers were hauling the biggest things they could carry to pile along the front of the ugly dam.

Please, God, let it hold.

The water was still rising. Only the top few inches of the last flag remained visible above water.

Ray kicked his way through the ankle-deep water until he got to Aaron. "Looks like our estimates were about right. Another hour and that last flag will be underwater."

"Good thing too. I don't think our people can last much longer."

"We're almost done. Mike and I sent most of the women and Some of the men inside. Speaking of which, Aaron, you don't look so great yourself. Why don't you go in and lay down?"

"I wish I could. I have to stay sharp for these people, and..."

Two women staggered to them. One had an arm draped over the shoulder of the other. "Help us. My friend stepped on a nail or something digging through the rubble. It went clear through her foot."

Ray put an arm around the woman's waist. She put her arm over his shoulder.

Aaron squatted down and looked at the injury. "This confounded rain is washing away the blood, but I think your foot is still bleeding. Whatever you stepped on was bigger than a nail." He stood and joined Ray in supporting the woman. "We need to get you inside so Ben can dry it off and get a better look."

The woman's face twisted in pain as she clung tightly to the shoulders of the men. "Thank you."

Mike looked over. "What happened to her?"

Aaron tightened his grip on the lady's waist. "She stepped on something that punctured her foot. We're taking her inside. Are you almost finished?"

"As good as we can. Here come the guys with the last wagon load."

From across the street, three men were hauling Aaron's garden wagon through the water. The water half-way up the wheels. One man pulled while the other two pushed.

Aaron called into the garage. "Go get Ben."

Sandy and Mason were at the door. Mason picked up the woman, and carried her inside to the tent. Aaron turned around and went back outside.

Ray motioned at the rising water. "We're out of time."

Aaron looked where Ray was pointing. The water was slapping at the edge of the dam.

Mike joined the two. He ran his open hand across his face flicking off the water. "This is a jury-rigged construction." He repeated the wipe across his face. "I don't think it'll hold for long."

Aaron spit loose water off his lips. "How long?"

"Best guess—three or four hours."

Aaron ran his hand over the face of his watch. "It's five o'clock now. It'll be dark about the time the house floods. Before then, we need to feed everybody. After that we'll get out the ladder and start moving people onto the roof.

Ray used his hand to shield his eyes and stared at the roof. "We have two injured people who can't climb anything. Some of the others are too old or too heavy to get up a ladder. We gotta rig a hoist."

Aaron gestured toward the metal shelving at the side of the garage. "I know. I still have some rope left. Maybe we can tie it to the corners of the last heavy tarp to make a sling."

"If we don't fall off the roof while we're hauling 'em up."

Aaron put his hands on his hips. "We won't worry about it until after they've eaten. We'll have to tell our people the dam won't hold."

Ray nodded in agreement. "I'll give Mason a hand with the cooking. What're you going to do?"

"Call the command center."

Aaron patted Mike on the shoulder. "We couldn't have done this without you. Go on inside and relax."

"You don't have to tell me twice."

Aaron walked to his golf cart parked inside the arc of the dam. He slipped into the seat and pulled out his radio. "Command center, this is Aaron. Come in." He tried three more times before he got an answer.

"Command center to Aaron. This is Scott. Sorry, I stepped away from the radio for a few minutes. What's your situation?"

Aaron briefly described the dam they'd built. "We finished just in time. Any minute the water will flood the top of the hill. I don't expect our dam will hold more than a few hours. After that, we'll get on my roof. I have two serious injuries. You'd better get some help to us soon. At least evacuate our injured."

Static popped and shrieked from the radio before Scott came back. "Conditions at the shelters we're managing have not improved. We're housing thousands and have hundreds injured. The weather is clearing from the south. We now have a steady flow of helicopters taking people to a refugee camp. But it'll still be awhile before we can help you."

Aaron squeezed the transmit button and snapped into the radio. "God damn it. Do you people intend to wait until we're dead and then stop by to fish our bodies out of the water? I've been talking to you for two days and all I've gotten is a bunch of nuthin'. I'm telling you, we're at the end. No place else to hide. Now somebody flip the emergency switch over there and get us some help."

"Wait one."

Aaron sat and watched the rain falling for what seemed like forever.

Finally, Scott was back on the air. "More than me are listening in. How much water is on the street in front of your house?"

"Maybe three or four inches. You can put a helicopter down here. We cleared out a lot of debris right in front of my driveway when we built the dam."

Aaron waited and waited, then keyed the transmit button again. "Are you still there?"

"Still here, Aaron. I was talking about your situation to some other people. The judgement is we won't be able to get a helicopter or any relief to you the rest of today.

Aaron exploded. "You, assholes. Let me spell it out for you. Our flimsy little dam is only going to hold for a few hours. I gotta get my people onto the roof while there's still light enough to see. About half the old people here won't be able to climb a ladder without help, to say nothing of our injured. Even if we get everyone on the roof, they'll still have to lay exposed to the weather and the rain for hours. Some of them may not survive. They're beat to pieces, tired, wet, and cold. Unless you heartless bastards do something, you'll be collecting corpses when you finally get off your asses."

There was another long pause. Eventually Scott came back.

"I'm very sorry. We'll get there as soon as we can. Try to hold out until we do."

Aaron took a deep breath and tried to calm himself. "I shouldn't shoot the messenger, but what is it you're not telling me?"

"Conditions here are over the top critical. The same helicopters you need, are already picking people off roofs. Not everyone was as well-prepared as you. In fact, we are using your group as the standard for others. When people scream about us not helping them, we give you as an example. You've been running a rescue operation on your own, with no help at all and, until now, haven't complained once."

"We won't be an example much longer. We really are close to the end."

"The storms are moving north. It's starting to clear in Orlando and Tampa Bay. We expect it to stop raining on you during the night. The flood waters will be falling by tomorrow morning. Tell that to your people."

Chapter 23
Escape to the Roof

<u>Sundown, Wednesday</u>

Aaron leaned against the frame of the garage door watching the continuing deluge. The flood waters washed against the arc of the dam. He estimated the water had risen two feet or more against the makeshift barrier. It was already leaking and water was creeping up the narrow slope of the driveway toward the garage. Aaron shook his head at the ominous sight.

The two-dozen refugees of the disaster sat on the few chairs or slumped against the walls of the garage. They put on the dry clothes left in the garage when they went outside to build the dam, passing soggy towels between them to wipe away the water from their hair, face, and body. They were sullen and cheerless. There was very little conversation. Most of them still had their empty paper plates in their laps, too tired to make the effort to throw them away.

Angie handed her husband a plate of food. "You need to eat. You're the last one."

Aaron looked at the plate. There was half a hot dog, a couple pieces of cooked roast, a small mound of pasta and a little corn. "I get what's left?"

"No, you got the same as everyone else. That's all there is."

"Slim rations for hungry people."

"They wouldn't have anything if you hadn't taken them in."

Aaron put his hands on Angie's shoulders and whispered into her ear. "The worst is yet to come. The dam's failing. When it goes, we'll flood. Before then, we have to get everyone except the injured up the ladder and onto the roof."

"What are you gonna do, leave them behind?"

"Hardly, but my backup plan is almost as desperate."

"Nobody's coming?"

"Not tonight. Maybe by tomorrow morning the rain will

stop, and they'll be able to send some help our way."

"You better get everybody moving."

"Right."

"Giving them something to eat will make your scheme easier to swallow, so to speak."

Aaron didn't answer. He crooked a finger at Ben, who was moving among the people giving them first-aid, pain pills and words of comfort. He came over when he saw Aaron's signal.

"I haven't been able to talk with you for a while, Doc. How's the lady with the bad leg?"

"Not good. Whatever she stepped on, seriously tore her up. I got the bleeding stopped with a tourniquet but if she doesn't get some real care very soon, she might lose her foot."

"What about Mark?"

"Okay, as long as he lays quiet."

"We gotta move him."

"Where?"

"On top of the counters in the kitchen. When the house floods, the water may not get that high."

"You hope."

"Yeah, I hope. I can't think of any other way. Stand with me while I talk to everyone."

Aaron stepped into the middle of the garage. Ben went with him. Mason joined them from the grill. The garage went quiet.

"The storms are ending. My guy at the command center says it's clearing in Orlando and Tampa Bay. It should stop raining sometime during the night. By sunup, they'll be able to do something to evacuate us."

Sighs of relief and weak cheers filled the garage.

"Until then, we have to keep us safe. We bought ourselves some time with our dam. It won't hold for long. When it fails, the garage and house will flood. We have to get every everybody onto the roof.

The sighs turned to groaning and grumbling.

Aaron spread his hands out in understanding. "I wish there was another way, but there isn't. I've put up a ladder to the roof, around the corner from the garage door. I want to get the men up the ladder first with more at the bottom to push others up. We'll rig a rope sling to secure those who need help climbing the ladder."

Ray had a rope coiled in his hands as he joined Aaron. "All you have to do is put this loop under your arms and the rest of us will pull you up, nice and easy."

Mike motioned to the men who had helped build the dam, and they headed outside.

Ray threw the rope over his shoulder and handed the men lanterns, flashlights and umbrellas as they went by.

When the rest of the survivors didn't stir, Aaron raised his voice. "I said move people. We can't waste a single second."

Mason walked forward and beckoned at the two men wearing coveralls. They moved toward the open garage door. He put his hands on the shoulders of two others, and the five stepped into the rain.

Aaron pulled out his last tarp from a storage bin. He turned to the women still in the garage. "Angie will go up with you. When you get to the roof, use this tarp to keep the rain off your heads. The faster you can get up the ladder and onto the roof, the sooner you will be under cover." He handed Angie the tarp. She went over and took one of the women by the arm. With Angie in the lead, they moved toward the open garage door.

Aaron flipped up his coverall hood and looked to see the progress of getting people up the ladder to the roof. "You ladies can wait till we get the men up. No reason to get wet until you have to."

A couple of the men needed the rope sling to help them climb the ladder with Ray and another man pulling them up. When the ladder was clear, Aaron nodded at Angie. She led the way, brushing past Aaron on the way out. "What about you?"

"I'm going to help Ben and Amy move our injured to the kitchen."

Before Aaron could take a step, there was a sharp grinding sound from the driveway. He looked around. The force of the water behind the dam was pushing the golf carts knocking them out of line. The dam was failing. Water was beginning to pour through the open spaces.

"Hurry," screamed Aaron. "It'll be knee-deep in minutes."

Angie pushed the women out the door. They huddled around the bottom of the ladder. Ray dropped the rope down and Angie put it under the arms of a heavy woman. Between the men pulling from the roof and pushing at the base of the ladder, they raised her up, her feet slipping from rung to rung. The other women went up nearly as fast.

Aaron grabbed Mason and handed him the two-way radio. "Take this with you and listen for calls from the command center."

Mason gave him a surprised look, but then nodded. "There's less interference on the roof than down here."

"Put people under the tarp across the crest of the roof. I'm gonna give Ben and Amy a hand with our injured." He ducked back into the garage.

❖

Mason barely got to the base of the ladder when he heard a prolonged grinding and then the deafening sound of the entire structure of the dam giving way. A three-foot wall of water rushed toward him. He grabbed the ladder to keep it from washing away. Ray and another man hauled on the rope and pulled an older, frail woman bodily onto the roof.

Blue sparks danced around the base of the generator. Then it sputtered and stopped. A small ring of smoke gushed from the grill.

Mason yelled at Mike. "You guys get up the ladder. I'll keep it steady." He swung around to the back of the ladder and held on as Mike and the others scrambled up the rungs. The rushing water rose past his knees and half-way up his thigh.

When the weight of the last person lifted, Mason could feel the base of the ladder slipping away. It crashed to the side, splashing and disappearing under the water. He turned around and put his hands on the side of the garage trying to brace himself to keep from falling into the water. As he struggled, the rope sling swung down from the roof.

Ray leaned over the edge and hollered down. "Grab on, Mason, we'll pull you up."

Mason snatched the swinging rope and pulled it over his head and under his shoulders. It took three men to hoist his dead weight over the gutter. As his chest fell on the roof, more hands reached down and pulled him up by his shorts. The rough treatment wrenched the staples on his butt and leg. He winced as he fell onto the wet shingles.

Ray held an umbrella over him as he helped him to his feet. "Are you okay?"

"Mostly. I think I jerked out some sutures when you pulled me up."

"More than a couple. Look at the blood running down your leg."

Mason didn't want to look. He knew what had happened. "Not much we can do about it now. Our Doc is underneath us in the garage or the kitchen. I sure hope they're all right."

"Me too. When the dam gave way, a ton of water flowed in there."

"Not much we can do about that either. Did you get everyone under the tarp?"

"All the women and most of the guys. The rest of us are using these umbrellas. Let me give you a hand."

Mason put an arm around Ray's shoulders. With every move, darts of pain shot up his back. The two of them shuffled up the roof to the peak where the tarp draped over the drenched

survivors. Light spilled out the edges from the lanterns. He looked
up at the sky. The sun was setting and the darkness deepened.

Great place to spend the night.

Mason dropped to his knees and peeked under the tarp.
The women were in a group at the center with men clustered
around them. The tarp didn't cover everyone. A few of the men sat
close to the edge, getting a little relief from the rain with three or
four umbrellas. They were a sorry bunch. Besides being wet to the
bone, the climb to the roof looked like it had used the last of their
strength. They huddled together, leaning on each other for
support.

Mason spotted Angie. "Everyone present and accounted
for?"

"I think so. If someone were missing, we'd know it. I know
Aaron isn't here."

"He's helping Ben and Amy with our injured. I hope they
got them out of the tent and onto the kitchen counters before
water poured into the house."

"They're stuck down there, aren't they?"

"Like we're stuck up here. The water knocked down the
ladder. I was the last up."

Angie scooted closer to Mason. "There's blood running
down your leg. You must have pulled your staples getting up
here."

"Some of 'em, anyway."

"That's gotta hurt."

"I'm trying to ignore it."

When the dam gave way, Aaron was standing by the garage
door. A gush of water rushed toward him. He dashed into the
kitchen. Several inches of water flowed across the floor before he
got the door shut. Even then, water was leaking in around the
door frame after the deluge plowed into it.

Ben and Amy lifted the lady with the slashed foot onto a

counter. Ben looked up. "Glad we got some dry blankets from the tent to put under these people on the counters, before they got soaked. Help me bring the man with the bad back in here."

The two went into the tent. The injured man was lying on the floor, lifting his head to keep the water from getting in his nose and mouth. Ben and Aaron picked him up as gently as they could. He screamed in pain as they carried him into the kitchen and laid him down on some blankets folded on the counter.

Ben shoved Aaron into the laundry room. Amy followed them, sliding the door closed.

There was a look of desperation in Ben's eyes as he spoke softly to Aaron. "Almost all my medical supplies and drugs are gone. I don't have anything more for pain. I hope we didn't get new injuries when people moved to the roof."

Aaron shrugged. "I've no idea what's going on up there. There's no way to help them, even if you had medicine and bandages. We can't get out, and they can't come down. We're stuck until someone comes to rescue us."

"How long will that be?"

"All night long, for sure. I gave the radio to Mason. He can see what's happening from the roof better than me. Nineteen of our twenty-four people are up there with him."

Amy put a hand on Aaron's arm. "How deep is the water outside?"

"Three or four feet. It won't be long before it gets in here. We can only hope it doesn't rise above the counter tops."

Ben headed for the door. "Until then, I've got some injured people to care for." When he slid the door open, dirty water surged into the laundry room rising halfway to his knees.

As Aaron sloshed through the water, there was a loud crack. He lifted his head to follow the sound. A long fracture went the length of the kitchen ceiling and down the wall leading to the garage.

Aaron grimaced. "I hope the house holds together.

Chapter 24
Catastrophe

Mason heard the ceiling crack. He also felt it. The entire roof shuddered beneath his feet. He put a hand down to steady himself. Ray was crouching nearby.

Mason looked up at him. "That was a hell of a jolt. I'm surprised the rest of the house didn't fall down."

"It may yet. The house took a beating from the hurricane. Don't think what's left can stand much more."

There was a scream from the tarp. Both Mason and Ray shuffled over and looked under it. A space had opened in the center with a woman lying there. A sobbing man knelt before her.

Mason pulled on the arm of a man sitting outside the tarp, seeming oblivious to the rain drenching his head and running down his shoulders. "What's happened?"

"That lady over there is dead. We thought she had passed out, but when somebody checked her, there was no pulse. I got out of there."

Ray worked his way under the tarp and around people until he got to the woman. He put his fingers to her neck. After a moment, he shook his head and motioned for Mason.

When Mason joined him, Ray signaled for him to feel for a pulse while he put his ear to the woman's chest, then lifted her eyelid. The others under the tarp watched them, shock, disbelief, and fear on their faces.

Within a minute, Ray and Mason looked at each other. Ray spoke in a murmur. "Got anything?"

"Nothing. How about you?"

"I didn't hear a heart beating. Pupils fixed and dilated. I think she's gone."

Mason grimaced, then leaned over and whispered in Ray's ear. "We gotta get her out of here. These people are freaking out."

Ray nodded and scooted around to grab the woman by the

shoulders. Another man got her legs, and they dragged her out of the cover of the tarp. The crowd gave them a wide berth. Some of the women were crying. They carried her to an open space farther down the slope of the roof. Mason was glad to get some help. He didn't think his throbbing wound could stand anymore. He crawled out into the open and stood up next to Ray.

Mason stared at the dead woman lying obscenely in the rain. "I'm going to call the command center and give them a report." He walked a few steps away and held an umbrella over his head while he pulled out the radio.

"Mason to command center. This is Aaron's site. Anybody there?"

Immediately, he got a response. "This is Scott. What's your situation?"

"Our dam has collapsed, and water is in the garage and house. We've gotten our survivors onto the roof. We have another fatality."

"I'm sorry. Where's Aaron?"

"He stayed in the house to help our doc and his wife handle our other injured people. I'm sure they're up to their asses in water. I've no idea what kind of mess you have there, but I'm telling you we have eighteen people stranded in the rain on the roof and five more in the house. If you don't get some help in here pretty damn quick, it'll be too late."

There was only static on the radio for a moment before Scott came back. "How deep is the water around your house?

"Two or three feet, at least. Much deeper down the hill."

"Hold a minute."

It seemed a lot longer than a minute before Scott came back. "We now have a couple of pontoon boats I think we can get in there, at least close enough for your people to wade to the boats."

"How long will that take?"

"They have to work around a lot of debris. Two or three

hours, at least."

"Get 'em movin'."

"Roger. Help is on the way. Tell your people, and hold out till we get there. If anything else happens, call me back."

Mason acknowledged and clicked off. He shuffled to the crest of the roof where Ray was sitting. "The command center is sending pontoon boats." He glanced at his watch. "Figure about three hours."

Ray looked at his own watch. "Not before ten o'clock. Still, knowing help is coming should make it easier for these poor people. I'll go tell them."

Mason walked over to the edge of the roof. He couldn't see the ladder. He would have to jump off the roof, hunt for it under the water, and set it back up to give the survivors a way down.

Easier said than done.

Aaron had troubles of his own. When the rafters in the roof cracked, water found a way into the house. Now he had a rainstorm inside the kitchen and garage. Water ran down the slope in the kitchen ceiling and dripped in a hundred places. The same was true for the garage. A monstrous stench rose from the filthy water. It had now risen well above his knees. To make matters worse, the sound of menacing cracks from the rafters continued to echo through the room.

Ben held his hand to his head to keep water out of his eyes. "Give me a hand, Aaron. I need to get Mark pushed under the overhang of the cupboards."

The suffering man clenched his jaws as the two eased him to a drier spot.

Aaron cocked his head toward the injured woman. "What about her?"

"She scooted herself undercover."

Aaron walked over and looked into her eyes. Her face blanched white. "I'm sorry we can't do more for you. We hope to get you out of here when help comes."

"It can't be too soon."

"In all the turbulence, I've never learned your name."

"It's Susan. Is my husband okay?"

"Think so. He went up on the roof with the others."

Aaron was at a loss for more to say. He turned back to Ben and gave him a questioning look. Ben shook his head. His shoulders were slumped in helplessness.

On an impulse, Aaron waded to the kitchen door and opened it. His heart sunk as he looked at the stinking water which filled his garage. Nothing remained of the well-ordered workspace he used to have. Hunks of wood, plastic bottles, pieces of vegetation, and the corpses of animals floated across the surface.

Aaron retched as he worked his way to the open garage door. He swung around the corner of the house and hollered up to the roof. "Can anyone up there hear me?"

A moment later, Mason peered out over the edge, rain pouring from his head. "Looks like the house flooded. Are you guys okay?"

"It's still dry on the counter tops. We put our injured up there. We're stable for the moment. What's going on up there?"

"One of the women died. I talked to the command center and told them the rest of our people were soaking wet on the roof. They sent a couple of pontoon boats to evacuate us."

"Best news I've heard today. How long will it take to get to us?"

"They said about three hours. I wouldn't count on that. There's no telling what kind of obstacles they'll run into."

"Where's the ladder?"

"It fell over when the dam broke. It's under the water. Can you feel around with your feet and find it?"

Aaron shuffled his feet in the water, feeling for the ladder. He knew where it had been and was annoyed he couldn't find it. Finally, his foot hit something solid. It was the ladder. He leaned over and felt with his hands, trying to keep the foul water out of his mouth. The job of fishing it out and leaning it back against the gutter took a long time. When he finished, Aaron put his hands on the side of the house and gasped air to catch his breath. It should have been easy to do, yet it nearly exhausted him.

Mason watched Aaron struggle to raise the ladder. He clicked on a flashlight and shined it into Aaron's face. "You look like you're running on the last drop in the tank."

"Nothing a decent meal, and three days of sleep wouldn't fix." Aaron climbed a few rungs up the ladder to get out of the water. "I don't suppose you have a spare umbrella?"

"What for?"

"The ceiling inside is leaking."

"Not surprised. When the rafters cracked, the whole roof shifted. It jarred us all."

"The cracks and creaks and sounds of splintering wood haven't stopped since the first big crash. I'm afraid the roof will collapse."

"That ain't good. We'd better get everyone out from underneath it."

"We have to figure a way to get our injured up there. If we move Mark again, we could hurt him worse than he already is."

"Better than him being crushed if the roof falls in."

The words were barely out of Mason's mouth before the thunderous sound of wood cracking, and splintering filled the air. The roof dropped out from under his feet. Mason fell on his face, digging his fingernails into the shingles to keep from sliding off the roof into the water.

Ray ran over and grabbed his arms. "The outside walls of the house buckled out."

Mason jumped to his feet. "Aaron was on the ladder."

He shined his light into the dark waters. Concrete blocks littered the surface from the front of the garage to the back of the kitchen. Only a small part of the ladder was above the water. A hand gripped one of the rungs.

Ray pointed. "There he is."

Mason slipped off the roof and into the water, Ray went with him. The two got to each side of the ladder and began pushing concrete blocks away. Mason grabbed Aaron's hand, pulling his arm. Aaron's head came out of the water. Mason cradled one arm around Aaron's shoulders as he furiously pulled at the blocks pinning the helpless man under the water. Ray was doing the same on the other side. Within seconds, they cleared away enough rubble to pull Aaron out and lift him onto the roof. Mike and another man stepped down the slope of the roof to the water's edge and pulled Aaron the rest of the way.

Mason climbed out of the water first and crawled over to Aaron. He was not breathing. "I'm gonna start CPR."

For several desperate moments, Mason alternated between pushing his hands against Aaron's chest and blowing air into his mouth. At last, Aaron began coughing up water, and he started to breathe.

Ray felt around Aaron's head. "There's a big gash back here. I can't tell how much he's bleeding. The rain is washing it away."

Mason nodded grimly. "He's unconscious. Help me drag him up, so we can get the tarp over his head and out of the rain."

Only one side of the roof had collapsed. It made the angle much steeper under the fallen outside wall. That edge of the roof was now underwater. The survivors had scampered to the other side of the roof and were clinging to the crest. Mason and Ray pulled Aaron to the peak laying him as close to the top as they could.

Mike scooted over to the two. "How bad is he hurt?"

Mason shook his head. "Don't know. All I can see is the cut on his head. He could be bleeding inside." He grabbed a wet towel and put it under his head.

Ray started feeling down Aaron's body. "Those coveralls cover everything up. I... just a minute." He ran his hands down Aaron's legs. "I think his leg is broken below the knee. If it's a compound fracture, he could be bleeding there.

Ray pulled the coverall leg up so he could see. It was a compound fracture. A broken bone jutted out from the skin on Aaron's leg. Blood dripped from the gash.

Mason motioned to Mike. "Get a hold of his shoulders while Ray tries to pull his leg back in place.

Ray clenched his jaw as he put his hands around Aaron's ankle and gave a sharp tug. The bone snapped back into place, but his leg continued to bleed. "It's a good thing he's still unconscious. I wish Ben were up here."

Mason wiped water from his face. "So do I. I hope he and the others didn't get crushed when the roof fell in."

"Only half the roof collapsed. Maybe it missed them."

"Then, where are they?"

Ray was about to answer when the sharp crack of breaking wood came at the same time the rest of the roof crashed down in a heavy thud.

Everyone screamed as the sudden drop jolted them. People grabbed each other to keep from sliding into the water. Mason threw himself onto Aaron to keep him from slipping away.

He lay there for a moment stunned at the depth of the catastrophe. He clenched his jaw and shook his head.

Ray crawled over and put a hand on his back. "I'm sorry, Mason. I don't think anyone is coming out now."

The rain mixed with Mason's tears.

Chapter 25
Fighting to Survive

Mason tried to concentrate. Sandy's voice floated across to him.

"Mason... Mason. Look at me, honey."

Mason raised his head and stared into the eyes of his wife. "They're gone, Sandy. Ben, Amy and our injured were inside when the roof fell in."

"I know. There was nothing any of us could do, including you."

"Yeah ... yeah. It doesn't make it easier." He looked down at Aaron. "Dad is still unconscious. The gash in his head has stopped bleeding. We found some floating wood to use as a splint for his broken leg."

"What can I do?"

"Stay with him. Talk to him. Tell him he's gonna be okay."

"Think he can hear me?"

"I've seen it before with guys who got shot to pieces and survived. They say it made a big difference hearing an encouraging voice speaking to them, even if they were out of their mind with pain and panic."

"What are you gonna do?"

"Gotta call the command center. I hope the damn radio works. It got wet when I jumped in the water."

Mason shuffled to a far corner of the remaining roof. He turned his back to everyone and unzipped his coverall, pulling the radio off his belt. It was wet, but the red light went on when he flipped the switch.

He pushed the transmit button. "Mason to command center."

Immediately there was a response. "This is Scott, Mason. I've been trying to call you for over an hour."

"I turned off the radio to save the battery."

"What's your situation?"

"The roof collapsed. Our doc, his wife and our two injured were under it."

"Any chance they're still alive?"

"Very unlikely. There's no way for me to even look."

"I'm so sorry."

"What's the latest on boats to rescue us?"

"I wish I had better news. The boats went out, but they couldn't find their way through the debris in the dark. We'll have to wait until it gets light to try again."

"What are we supposed to do until then?"

"Do you have any other injuries?"

"Aaron is still unconscious. Everyone was rattled when the roof went down, but I don't think anybody else is hurt." Mason paused briefly. "These people are wet and cold from exposure. They're exhausted and weak. They need to be evacuated."

"At first light, we'll start out again. I'm going with them this time."

"I thought you were running the com link?"

"There are several of us on the radio. I've been talking to isolated groups. We've rescued or lost contact with all but yours."

Mason struggled to remain calm. "That means you can give us your full attention. It's about time. We've been fighting to stay alive for two days. We've lost six people in this disaster, but we have eighteen stuck on what remains of this roof. You guys need to do something."

"We will and we are. Hold on for a few more hours."

"You're not just saying that? I gotta go back and tell these people, who are almost at the end of their strength, they have to sit underneath a wet canvas until tomorrow morning."

"I can only imagine what you've been through. We're ready to launch a full-scale rescue."

Mason took a deep breath and looked up at the dark skies. "Roger, out."

Gritting his teeth from the pain, Mason crabbed back

across the roof. All he could make out in the dark was the tarp, which looked like a misshapen tent from the people underneath it. Sandy peaked out from an edge and pointed a flashlight to help Mason. Ray was watching too. Both scooted out to meet him.

Sandy gave her husband a hug. "What did you find out?"

"The boats had to turn back. They couldn't see their way around the debris floating in the water. We'll have to wait until morning."

Ray gave a little nod. "I didn't think there was much chance they would make it tonight. What are you going to say to the others?"

"Help them remember what they've done together makes them stronger. Aaron was able to turn the I into We, and the Me into Us. We can't lose that."

Mason didn't wait for a response. He lifted an edge of the canvas. The lanterns cast shadows across the people, now packed together. Every eye focused on him.

"I've spoken to the command center. The boats can't get to us in the dark, but they promise to send them out again at dawn."

Groans, moans, and whimpers sounded from everyone under the dripping canvas.

Mason went on with earnest resolve. "Now, listen to me. We've shared our food and dry clothes. We worked to build our dam. It bought us the time we needed to hold back the water. We did these things working together, functioning as a team. It's saved so far. Now, we have to wait a little longer, but we're still a team."

The clustered survivors gloomily lowered their heads, but looked up as Mason launched into a bawdy sea shanty. He wasn't very musical and sang off-key, but the others smiled at the catchy words. When he finished, Sandy started a tune of her own. More recognized this song and began singing along. One melody merged into another, and soon the entire group was singing at the top of their lungs.

Ray cast a glance at Mason and smiled. "That'll keep 'em busy for a while." He slipped under the canvas and added his own voice to the chorus.

Sandy and Mason sat under an umbrella at the edge of the canvas. Mason muttered to her. "When they run out of songs, start them talking about relatives, family, children, grandchildren—anything to keep their minds off what they're enduring."

"I know a bunch of songs. I'll keep 'em going."

"You do that, honey. It might seem silly, but I've seen this before in combat situations. The enemy here is the weather. Living through this disaster, as a group, makes self-sacrifice look less important. Individuals live on through the lives of their comrades."

"I'll take your word for it. I can't remember you telling me anything about your overseas deployments."

"If you tell an experience, you have to live through it again. For the guys who really did it, that's the last thing they want to do."

Random melodies floated out from under the canvas. "Sounds like our folks are starting to repeat themselves. I'll go teach them some new songs."

Mason nodded as Sandy ducked back under the canvas.

The music calmed Mason. He settled onto the shingles, put his head down, closed his eyes, and drifted into sleep.

An absence of sound caused Mason to stir. He glanced at his watch—nearly midnight. He'd been asleep for almost two hours. The singing had stopped, but there was something else. It took a moment for him to figure it out. He put out his hand. Only light drizzle was falling on his palm.

The rain's stopping.

He looked up to the sky. The heavy clouds parted and he could see stars. Another bank of clouds drifted past, and a full moon gleamed down on the rooftop. It was big, and round, and silver—and perfect. Mason's spirits rose.

When he lifted the edge of the canvas and looked underneath. Most of the people were also sleeping. They were leaning on each other. Some of the wives had their heads in the laps of their husbands.

Mason touched Sandy gently on the shoulder. She came awake instantly. "What is it?"

"Something good for a change. Come on out. You won't need to pull up your coverall hood. The rain has stopped."

"Has it? That is good news." Sandy skidded into the open and looked at the moonlit sky. "What a glorious sight. I never thought I would be so glad to see the moon."

"Everyone else will feel the same."

"What about Dad?"

"He hasn't regained consciousness. I'm so worried about him."

"We'll be able to get him medical care in a few hours. For sure, the boats will reach us shortly after dawn."

The radio crackled to life. "Scott calling Mason, over."

Mason unzipped his coverall and pulled out the radio. "Mason here. With the skies clearing, I hope you guys can get an early start."

"There's enough moonlight for us to see to load up. We'll get moving as soon as there's light. What's your situation?"

"Aaron is still out cold. There's no way to tell how bad he's hurt other than a busted leg. Otherwise, we've been able to get some sleep. How long do you figure it will take you to reach us?"

"It can't be more than a couple miles from the command center to you. Assuming we can find our way through the floating junk, we'll get there quickly."

"Don't suppose the clearing weather will let you get some helicopters in here?"

"Everybody in central Florida is screaming for helicopters.

The few we've gotten, brought food, water, and medical supplies and evacuated our seriously injured. The damage is so extensive emergency equipment is strained to the limit. These pontoon boats are the best we can do."

"Okay. Get 'em moving as fast as you can."

Sandy pointed to the canvas. "Let's get that thing off our people. We'll have more room and maybe we can even start drying out a little."

Ray joined the two while they were talking. "I heard that. Give me a hand."

Sandy and Ray flipped the tarp off the huddled survivors. Sandy sang out. "Hey everybody. Things are looking up. See for yourself."

As the moonlight shone down, eyes turned to the sky and people pointed. "It's stopped raining ... Great to see the moon and a clear sky ... I can see my shadow."

Mason broke into a wide grin. "I have more good news. I spoke to the command center. They're getting ready right now. As soon as the sun comes up, the boats will head our way. Our rescue is only a few hours away."

Cries of relief rose from the rooftop.

Mason laughed. "That's the spirit. If I had a pot and some coffee, I'd set the roof on fire to heat it up."

It was a far-fetched idea, but the image it conjured up made everyone laugh. Mason laughed again too. He was glad to divert attention away from the delay of the arrival of the boats. "Since you can see what you're doing from the full moon, and in the absence of coffee and breakfast, this would be a good time to peel of some layers of wet clothes and wring them out."

With no attention to modesty, people pulled off their dripping shirts and pants and squeezed water onto the shingles.

The remainder of the night bubbled with brighter conversations. Having a sense their ordeal was nearly over, made the exchanges much more optimistic.

Mason stood away from the others and watched them as the night passed. He was the first to see the skies growing lighter, but not the first to shout out when the sun dawned on the horizon.

Everyone stood up to look at their shattered neighborhood. Only a few shredded palm trees were still standing. Shells of homes poked out of the water. The roof of Aaron's home, at the top of the hill, was the only refuge in sight. Mason knew the survivors would realize how fortunate they were. He also knew Aaron's prior planning along with tons of common sense were the reason they were alive.

Ninety minutes later, horns sounded in the distance. At last, the pontoon boats came into view, creeping slowly through the floating rubble. Men stood at the front of the boat and pushed debris aside with long poles.

A mighty cry rose from the men and women on the rooftop. They waved wildly at the boats,

Mason glanced around him. The water was falling fast. Already the top of the driveway was visible. The pontoon boats beached themselves in the street. Men jumped from the boats and helped everyone, who could, wade to the boats. There were stretchers for some of the others, including Aaron.

Chapter 26
A New Dawn

<u>Two days later</u>

Consciousness crept into Aaron's mind. He struggled to climb out of a deep pit. Gradually, waves of rational thought washed away the confusing clouds that engulfed him.

His first impression was a grinding pain at the back of his head and in his leg. The rest of his body ached from top to bottom. His eyelids flickered and opened.

Angie smiled at him and squeezed his hand. "Welcome back. You missed the best part."

Aaron cleared his throat and forced words out. "What I miss?"

"The part where the boats came and rescued everyone from the roof, including you. We had to haul you off on a stretcher."

"Sorry about that."

"You're alive. I forgive you."

Aaron looked across the room. Mason was in a bed next to him. He was asleep. "Is Mason okay?"

"He is now. He wanted them to patch him up and let him go. That wasn't going to happen. He lived with his injuries for four days. Plus, everything else he did, drained every ounce. They did some more surgery on his leg and butt. Since then, he's mostly slept."

"How long have I been out?"

"Two days. Mason and Ray pulled you out of the rubble. You broke your leg."

"The last thing I remember, was standing on the ladder when the roof caved in. Ben, Amy and our injured were inside the house. What happened?"

"They're dead, Aaron, and another woman died on the roof."

"Oh my God." Tears flooded Aaron's eyes. He turned his

bandaged head aside and sobbed.

"But we saved eighteen others. Some are still in hospitals. The last I heard they'll all make it."

Angie ran a towel over Aaron's cheeks. "The few of our bunch I've talked to say they're alive because of you. I'm sure the rest feel the same."

"They saved themselves."

Angie sat back in her chair. "I'm grateful we saved you. How do you feel?"

"Hungry, I think."

"Besides that."

"My body hurts all over, but my brain is pretty clear."

"Feel up to talking with someone?"

"It's not any media people?

"Haven't seen any of them. This guy's been waiting for you to wake up."

"All right."

Angie got up and went out the door. She was back in a moment. A burly man followed her into the room. "Aaron, this is Scott." Aaron smiled and put out a hand.

Scott came to the bed and took it, part in greeting and part compassion. "Howdy, Aaron. We talked on the radio so much, I feel like I know you."

"Good to put a face to the name. How about giving me a little briefing on what I've missed."

Scott settled into a chair next to the bed. "The news reports say this is the worst natural disaster in American history."

"No doubt. How bad?"

"After the hurricanes tore everything up, central Florida was flooded with four or five feet of rain. Rescue crews report deaths in the thousands. They're still plucking survivors off roofs."

"Like us."

"Most of them didn't make the preparations you did. It made a huge difference."

"We still lost six people."

"But a lot more did survive, including you. It's one of the best stories to come out of this tragedy. You did almost everything on your own, with no help from us."

Aaron turned his head aside. He didn't feel much like celebrating.

Scott changed the subject. "When things get back to normal, stop by and see me. In regular life, I'm the director of The Villages smart irrigation system."

Aaron laughed a little. "It's only smart if your sprinkler heads are not underwater. I imagine you have quite a bit of work to do."

"That's for sure." Scott got to his feet. "I don't want to wear you out. I just wanted to say hello."

"Thanks for waiting around for me, and thanks for helping me get through this."

Scott smiled and left the room.

As he was going out, Sandy came in and sat down at the side of the bed. She took her father's hand in hers. "Oh Daddy, I'm so glad you're awake."

"Gonna be okay."

From across the room, Mason grumbled. "You guys are making it hard to sleep."

Aaron looked across at him. "Well, wake up. The nightmare is over."

Everything about Phil Walker, his books, his approach to writing and interesting blogs may be found at philwalkerbooks.com

Enjoy these books by Phil Walker on Kindle

Killer Storms
Sanctuary In Time
The Black Angel
Crusade of The Black Angel
The Rangers are Coming
Lions and Tigers, and Bears, OH GOD!
Out of the Emerald Cathedral
The Magic and the Misery

The Starlight Series
The Holy Mission
The Galilee Foundation
The Galilee Garden
Island of the Angels
Terra Rising
Heaven's Angels
The Galactic Quest

Non-Fiction History

Visions Along the Poudre Valley
Modern Visions Along the Poudre Valley

Order paperback books from Amazon

The Black Angel
Crusade of The Black Angel
The Rangers are Coming
Sanctuary in Time
Killer Storms